THE MISSING BOY

CAROLINE BULLOCK

Copyright © 2025 by Caroline Bullock

First published 2025

Published by Chiselbury, a division of Woodstock Leasor Limited, 14 Devonia Road, London N1 8JH, United Kingdom

www.chiselbury.com

The moral right of Caroline Bullock to be identified as the author of this work is asserted.

This book is copyright material and must not be copied, reproduced, transferred, distributed, leased, licensed or publicly performed or used in any way except as specifically permitted by the publishers, as allowed under the terms and conditions under which it was purchased or as strictly permitted by applicable copyright law. Any unauthorised distribution or use of this text may be a direct infringement of the publisher's rights and those responsible may be liable in law accordingly.

All characters in this publication are fictitious and any resemblance to real persons, living or dead, is purely coincidental.

Cover design by Indra Murugiah

ISBN: 978-1-916556-63-8 (hardback)

ISBN: 978-1-916556-76-8 (paperback)

ISBN: 978-1-916556-64-5 (epub)

A CIP catalogue record for this book is available from the British Library.

Thanks to Peter Ritchie for his time given to help me with research on The Missing Boy

1

Maltham, England, June 2002

"Right, a young kid from Maltham prep has gone walkabout during his school jubilee procession. Leah, get onto the police press office; then over to the school, we need the name - see if you get anything out of the teachers there, oh, and find out if anyone around the high street saw anything."

She nodded, noting this rare charge of energy from her editor. Post deadline he usually requested a 'proper' cup of tea – in a pot with loose leaves – from his PA before hankering down in his office with the radio cricket commentary. Now he was waving his Mars Bar like a conductor's baton, jolting the collective lethargy of a newsroom that had also been killing time with a rolling tea round until 5pm.

Rifling through the carnage her desk, she found her latest notepad and checked the batteries in her Dictaphone.

He continued: "Oh and they're a right load of snooty bitches down there...."

"At the school?"

"Yep, a bloody nightmare at the best of times, prickly enough over sharing Ofsted results, so this will be very embarrassing for them. I doubt anyone will talk but it's worth a shot – at the very least you should find a parent hanging around with something to say, there always is at the place."

"So, was in his school uniform?"

"Nope, dressed as a St George knight apparently …. you know, chain mail helmets, white tabard with a red cross," he expanded noting the girl's blank face.

"Dressed as the St George knight," said his PA, Sue Lansford stirring in the corner. "Poor, poor little thing, four years old."

"He's not dead Sue," said the editor. "Or at least we don't know that – look, he might turn up in an hour in time for his tea, but then he might be in a ditch or with some pervert, either way we need to be prepared to do an updated late edition if necessary."

A brief pause and then murmurs began next door as the three sub editors digested the news and sloped through to join the impromptu briefing. Leah snidely observed their faces, weary with life and the dated sartorial concessions to the warmer weather, curious to see them away from the desks they were usually welded to.

"Now, I appreciate no one wants to start redoing the front page but we're going to look bloody stupid if we lead on the best dressed jubilee window while the first people hear of this is elsewhere," added the editor, keen to smother any dissent. "A missing four-year-old, this could be a big story - could go national."

It occurred to Leah that none of this needed to be explained but the experienced editor knew what he was doing and how to handle the awkward team he had to work with. Muted, compliant nods followed along with predictable theories on local perverts and broader musings around cost cutting at schools.

"Well, I know I wouldn't be happy paying prep school fees while they rely more and more on these new teaching assistants," said the chief sub-Sandy who in keeping with the established hierarchal conventions usually proffered an opinion first.

"Yes, it's a bit like these community police whatsits," agreed Sue.

"Those pretend policemen?" said Sandy.

"Exactly. Cheaper probably, but it's just not the same, not up to the job, no qualifications or proper training, just let loose in the classroom and then you start getting shortcuts and mistakes, it all follows. If you pay peanuts, you get monkeys."

"Why? Was a teaching assistant supposed to be looking after this kid?" asked Leah instantly regretting it.

"Leah, we know as much as you do at the moment which is sweet.... fanny...... Adams," responded the chief sub with the slow, weary tone she adopted for all their dealings. She rolled her eyes conspiratorially at Sue before turning back to Leah.

"It's called spec-u-lating."

As Leah had soon discovered, being new and under 30 was a sufficiently offensive combination to alienate much of the paper's crabby collective of sub editors and be precluded from what they considered to be their superior musings. In this regressive environment of bitter, old timers on poor pay, young people were there to be told off or tolerated, though Leah never felt inclined to complain or take them on, the small satisfaction derived from not being them providing enough one-upmanship for the time being.

"Messy desk, messy mind," someone muttered in the distance as the reporter churned though piles of payslips and press releases to find a spare battery for her Dictaphone. She grabbed her bag and water bottle and hurried out the room as distant moans over working late started to escalate now the subs were back in their own office.

The young woman paused on the stairs and listened, curious over whether the enthusiasm she felt for the job right now would remain or if these characters rattled by news daring to break at inconvenient times were the ghosts of her future. Either way, it was a reminder that she shouldn't stay here long; she had to soak up the good and spit out the rest and move on to a national newspaper before she became stifled by the lethargy around her.

Buoyed by this sudden and simple clarity of her life plan along with the frisson of a rare unfolding drama, the journalist felt a surge of satisfaction. It came as a newly acquired purpose that was absent throughout her driftless adolescence converged with a still pre-jaded youthful enthusiasm. The result was a hallowed time which sadly, like a golden era of music or a favourite icon's sporting reign, could never be appreciated at the time, but only missed when it was too late.

"Now, have you got *all of* your bits and pieces together? You haven't forgotten your notepad again, have you?"

Her editor was leaning over the banister a small, indulgent smile on his red face which along with his gentle nagging tone could make his seem more like a parent at times than a boss. She nodded and smiled, holding it up by way of proof, grateful as always for this simple prop which gave her an instant pass and excuse to access the thoughts and lives of strangers however briefly, removing the awkwardness she often felt without it.

Outside was another version of the airless heat which had consumed the office, this one faintly infused with barbecued meat and something sweet. Large flying ants, enough to be a nuisance swarmed close and she could see some police officers dotted down the pavements talking to members of the public. Out of sight, a distant patrol car's speaker appealing for information and repeating the boy's description slipped in and out of audibility.

Just an hour earlier, the scene had been colourful and decorative and packed with people enjoying the celebrations. Now, as dispersed crowds milled amongst the discarded flags, bunting and beer bottles, it had the faded glamour of a night club in the daytime when harsh light illuminates the stains, fag buts and upholstery tears.

A couple of teens sitting on the pavement with a pizza told her they had seen a minibus collect the rest of the school party but there was little else to go on in here and she was relieved to see the mayor and town clerk Gavin Smee talking to police outside the opticians.

As anticipated, this small hub had established itself as the epicentre of action and communication with plans for a volunteer search party under discussion in loud animated tones. She noticed the town clerk's jubilee window judging form was being used for an emergency shopping list featuring torches, batteries and water bottles. All was written in the hyper-neat handwriting Leah always associated with the dull and uncreative. Approximate costs were put at the side of each item in brackets, a solitary question mark next to the torches.

"Now I did check with the leader of the council, and we have the go-ahead to open the council chamber this evening as a base for the search party – I would suggest people convene there about six?" said Gavin.

One of the policemen nodded while the other added that an appeal for volunteers could be relayed via the car speaker that was circling the town.

"And the chamber will be a good refreshment point; there's plenty of space and it has a small kitchen with tea making facilities – a very large urn." added the town clerk writing teabags in capitals.

"Oh, Hi Leah." He turned to her and introduced her to the police, before relaying what had been discussed, scant details she already knew and lack of sightings and more interestingly the decision to close all surrounding road exits.

"So, you're treating it as an abduction?" the journalist asked the officer feeling the first prickle of adrenalin.

"We're keeping an open mind, but we'll be releasing a statement shortly and the press officer is your best port of call for now." The pair walked off quickly to talk to some approaching colleagues leaving the trio to chat among themselves.

"What a terrible, terrible business, to happen on today of all days – a day that had been so long in the making," said Gavin visibly more relaxed and open to gossip now that the officers had gone. "Someone will be up for the chop at Maltham Prep I would have thought - unbelievable. ..... I trust you'll be needing a quote from the town council and the mayor about all this?"

"What – the council's thoughts on the school's almighty cock up?"

"Oh, god no...." he touched her arm briefly as if to prevent her writing it down. "I was thinking about an official statement from the council expressing our concern."

She already knew this but just wanted to see his tight, little face looking panicked by the prospect of a rogue comment finding its way into the paper.

The journalist added: "You know it's all too late for our usual deadline with today being Thursday?"

"Of course, yes," he lied. "So, what will happen?"

"We're probably going to produce an emergency edition with an updated front page – which, sadly, means the best jubilee window spread maybe relegated."

"An emergency edition! That must be a first for the Herald," said the town clerk, a small smile forming as the beads of sweat along his upper lip started to trickle.

"Oh, don't worry about the jubilee window, of course this takes precedence," he added with a little swipe of the hand, missing the irony. She had forgotten that for someone who could laugh so readily at the lame jokes of his superiors, he had virtually no sense of humour.

News of an updated edition seemed to have heightened an already palpable air of excitement, sending both the mayor and town clerk's naturally officious pomposity and desire to be at the heart of any community drama in overdrive. As discussions resumed over the evening's plans, the cynic in her, suspected, it was an enthusiasm and performance emboldened by her appearance with both men keeping an eye on her notepad and moving nearer to ensure every idea and musing were picked up by her Dictaphone and reported.

Yet whatever their true agenda was, she wasn't that different. Heading out the office, she had swept pass the women on reception in a conflab with concerned looking locals and rolled her eyes at the talk of forecasted storms and how such a young child would soon be cold and scared. It had been the first time she had considered the child as a human being that could feel anything at all rather than simply a good story.

Outside she could see sun light and inside excessive and over emotional doom mongering. While she wished him no harm, he was primarily, an opportunity, viewed through the prism of her role, an attention-grabbing subject elevated from the usual fodder of planning appeals and traffic complaints with which she could make her mark, a bit of gravitas among the 100th birthdays and golden wedding anniversaries that were too often relied upon to fill the pages.

"Will you be covering the search party tonight?" Gavin asked her. "I think it would benefit from having a reporter there."

"Yes, I think will .... oh, what's the boy's name again?"

"Tom Steadman"

"Four years old, three foot three inches tall," added the mayor.

She wrote in her notepad and underlined the name twice.

2

Maltham, England, June 2017

The Maltham Herald, Page 1, June 12th, 2002
   By Leah Chase and Dave Garland
   Mystery surrounds the disappearance of four-year-old Maltham boy, Tom Steadman, who hasn't been since the afternoon of the Queen's Golden Jubilee celebrations in the town centre on Monday (June 9th)
   Dressed in a St George's Knight costume – the three-foot-tall youngster with dark curly hair was taking part in his school jubilee procession which was scheduled to finish at Yew Tree retirement home. Pupils had been expected to join the residents for a sit-down buffet of coronation chicken and Eton mess prepared by Maltham WI, but plans were aborted after the child was reported missing by the school...."

Stood in the musty chill of the paper's archive room, the well-thumbed 2002 edition in her hand, Leah smirked at the term 'mystery surrounds' remembering how the phrase had become a default start to a story low on facts and detail – through reporter ignorance or apathy or a bit of both.

As a junior reporter she hadn't been trusted to handle the write up alone, which is why senior writer Dave Garland had got involved adding quotes from people who saw nothing and pointless detail on buffets which sucked the life out of her original copy.

The grinning track-suited kid with side-parted dark curly hair stared out, shining, defiant eyes, forever linked to that hot celebratory Jubilee summer. Reliving it brought an odd comfort simply because it was rooted in nostalgia full of long forgotten details; the regular false 'sightings' from the time-rich that gave the boy a slightly absurd mythical status akin to black panther rumoured to stalk the county's woodlands, a bit of local folklore to fill space on a slow news day.

The case had defined Leah's stint at the paper as a new graduate the first-time round and 15 years later there was still very little to add, no body, no clues, no idea. His parents, David and Carolyn Steadman filled the rest of the pages – on holiday or at their large, detached home or various locations around Maltham - a photogenic affluence that had intensified and sustained public interest.

Groomed and attractive, there was no lank haired, dark eyed hollow stares, Cartier bands hung from tanned wrists and tasteful, expensive style prevailed throughout. Studying Carolyn's image for the first time in years, Leah was reminded of a woman fortunate enough to wake up pretty, leaning into the side of a well-built alpha husband, used to the easy comfort of being enveloped in a masculine arm. The picture was 15 years old, taken when she was in her prime and the journalist found herself curious and strangely hopeful of an inevitable physical decline of a woman she had never warmed to in spite of the circumstances.

She was at her desk now. Not her original position by the door, that caught the draft and unwanted enquires from reception but as a concession to her brush with greater things, the prime window seat with arm rests and high street view.

From here, she watched the comings and goings of Maltham's mainly white residents in their respective bubbles of life, taking sullen blazer-clad children for post school milkshakes, ignoring Big Issue sellers.

Some days, hours would pass like this – absorbed by very little and away from the editor's secretary and any real expectation for small talk, she had mastered the art of doing as little possible while appearing busy – pretending to make a call to avoid answering a real one, detaching herself more and more in this corner had become a welcome refuge. It suited her solitary disposition allowing her to write untaxing copy in peace and make the odd search online for higher paid jobs on the pretence that this situation was a fleeting stop gap rather than her new reality.

These were indeed strange times. She particularly hated dealing with tiresome enquiries from old contacts in the community and their expectations for answers and some kind of explanation. Those who remembered her leaving with a precocious swagger that came with a better offer now viewed her with suspicion, curious darting eyes trying to glean clues from her demeanour and weak, unconvinced smiles met her increasingly futile attempts to put a glossier spin on things.

With 15 years passing since the disappearance of Tom Steadman, the four-year old Maltham boy, last seen on the day of the Queen's Golden Jubilee, police admit the mystery may never be solved....

She paused distracted by an altercation between a car and cyclist and when her eyes returned to the screen, she wondered briefly how the words had got there. Medication was affecting her focus, numbing the creative edge as clichés and complacency crept in replacing the more original line of thought that had been her trademark. Her mind strained for a neater phrase, but it was all too much effort and so she persisted with more ordinary sentences she didn't have the capacity to improve.

3.30pm. The worst time of the day – when the tiredness of a medicated-sleep kicked in. The work experience boy appeared, and she found herself wondering what he looked like naked.

"The mayor's downstairs for you," said chief sub editor Derek Garland, another voice from the past. He had since been promoted from a pool of two to his current status which brought a negligible rise in pay and much more work.

The musty waft of cigarette and body odour embedded in the fibres of his mustard sweater worn regardless of season and circumstance was as she remembered as was the slow, croak testament to his 40 a day habit.

His yellow-tinged, crusty fingers fiddled with greasy hair, and she wondered if the jumper was ever washed, if he slept in it and more to the point, if he was still ensconced in the local bed and breakfast. She wasn't curious enough to inquire though and risk progressing their occasional exchanges beyond the bare minimum of a relayed message or query to any kind of conversation.

"Thanks," she said looking through her screen and feeling nauseous at his odour festering in the stuffy, airless newsroom.

She got up reluctantly but conceded that as visitors go Vince Dunkett was a more favourable option than most. She had always got on well with him and remembered when he had joined the council in 2002, she had warmed to his endearing rough edge. He stood out amid the pomposity of his council colleagues, who patronisingly referred to him as a 'a barrow boy' due to his East End roots, which remained a source of amusement to them as did anyone from the north. Plus, he always paid her compliments and bought good presents, and she liked people that did that.

3

Jean de Ruel, France, July 2017

Twinned with Maltham, the village of Saint Jean de Ruel in the Midi Pyrenees region of Southern France was elevated by a backdrop of fir-tree mountains and a majestic river that simultaneously purled and soothed.

Models of wolves, boars and beavers in grey slate stood along its banks indicating the presence of their real counterparts in nearby forests, a ferality on the fringes of a community of cute stone houses with pink and mint shutters where nothing escaped floral embellishment.

A chemist, hairdressers, tabac, bakery and doctors covered the modest essentials while the chimes of a 15th century church punctuated the rhythms and rituals of days in which no one seemed to be in much of a hurry.

Perhaps too subtle in its appeal to draw the masses, the place was however, catnip to those of a certain age and income. Untroubled by mortgages and life's work anxieties they bonded with their peers and locals over olive oil and honey stalls at the weekly markets and displayed a certain smug bonhomie-laced superiority that came from feeling 'in the know' and being privy to this this little-known idyll.

This conviviality continued over drinks and dinner at the village hotel, Le Midi de Nuit, a former 18th century coaching inn which usurped the church as the true nucleus of village life. The owners now in their fifth generation of the family sprang from its doors to collect fresh flowers or mussels from the fish man, a relentless work ethic and commitment to preserving the hotel's old-fashioned character rewarded by a loyal clientele who returned year after year, many spanning decades.

Leah was equally smitten. Sat in the elegant petit salon by reception thumbing a day-old Le Figaro, she was relieved that 15 years on her favourite bolthole was largely unchanged. It was still remarkably restrained in its concessions to the 21st Century – no lifts, a mobile phone ban throughout, which was mostly observed. The usual patronne now about 60ish greeted her with a flurry of pleasantries, her wiry frame betraying a strength that scooped up suitcases like handbags and strode up the two flights of stairs to show her to her usual room.

Hurrying to match her pace, Leah had a genuine admiration for those who did physical, drudgery with an enthusiastic disposition, so alien to her own lethargy.

"Voila mademoiselle", said Madame opening the window shutters with a flourish and releasing a waft of scented air and the river's roar into the little room.

The journalist particularly appreciated being addressed as Mademoiselle. It played to her ego and fragile mix of vanity and insecurity and confirmed that on cusp of 40 she looked much younger and could still convey the air of an ingenue at least in the eyes of some. In fact, how she was addressed in France had taken on an obsessive importance, a barometer of how good, or specifically how young, she was looking.

"Merci Madame, it's perfect," she said while being handed another large key for use of the separate bathroom down the corridor. It was the sort of quirk that would be unacceptable to her anywhere else, but here was simply a quaint anomaly she didn't really mind.

Standing on the balcony she absorbed the unchanged views of her usual spot and the clusters of pink-faced people traipsing across the bridge to the hotel for dinner.

The heat that had been so oppressive when travelling was now a comfort to her warming her skin as flutters of breeze curbed its intensity. There was an intimacy that came with the familiar, she thought, and with the promise of an evening of good food she felt a rare sense of calm and almost happiness.

These visits as part of Maltham Town Council's twinning activities were perhaps the only perk of returning to the local paper and with a particularly lax schedule this year she was looking forward to amusing herself most days, bar the odd event and evening dinner with rest of the party.

Here, feeling less judged, drained and stifled by past baggage she had more energy and optimism, elevated further by the high spirits of everyone she encountered. The result brought her a little closer to her the version of her old self when life was far less complicated, and she even had fun.

She considered having a quick walk around the village, but her clothes damp with sweat and stuck to her thighs and lower back signalled a wash was more important and there wasn't time for both. She fetched the key and her washbag and headed to the bathroom.

* * *

By now Saint Jean de Ruel was virtually deserted with the shut-up shop, pre-evening lull exodus, though laughter could be heard from behind shuttered houses.

In the silent, dark sanctuary of the church a man kneeled at the front pew his head bowed in prayer, the only witness a half-smiling statue of Saint Therese. He rose to his feet and lit a candle that stood tall amid the stubbier tealights and carefully arranged a photo of young boy of maybe two or three years behind it, bowing his head and making the sign of the cross.

Brushing away a tear he emerged back into the warm early evening air and made short walk back to his house.

It was no surprise to discover that Ros Cowley was still in her role at the council press office. It was the sort of steady, close to home, job for life she had always regarded as a major coup with a gratitude her employers had exploited ever since.

She never tired of telling people that she 'hadn't actually trained' in media relations but was proficient in a range of 'highly transferable' office skills, chiefly Excel spreadsheets. So impressed, apparently was the council with her enthusiasm for all things Excel that a decision was taken to overlook her lack of press release writing experience and give her the job. It was a leap of faith, Ros would say, that justified her lower than advertised salary that remained immune to any pay rise since and, thought Leah, whenever she heard this sorry spiel, explained why her press releases were laugh out loud bilge.

"Someone's looking very glamourous," said Ros, her default comment to anyone who wore a scrap of makeup.

Her great frame rose leaving an impression in the soft leather armchair, one of a few arranged round the cluster of coffee tables in the petit salon where guests had their aperitif.

"You look well Ros," Leah lied weakly enduring the moist hug that followed.

Ros was bare faced as usual, clear, soft unlined skin plumped more by virtue of her surplus four stone in weight than diligent skin care. The effect gave her, in her early 40s, the look of a giant baby. Her features looked smaller than ever, eyes like pin pricks, her tiny owl mouth and hamster teeth in contrast to hands like plates that were flapping theatrically in an attempt to cool herself down.

"Oh, God where's my handheld fan," she said churning the contents of her cheap, pleather handbag.

Leah put down her Burberry holdall, a present to herself when she landed the job on the national newspaper. She cast a pitying eye over Ros in her usual draping layers, a long skirt, baggy top and some sort of patterned scarf balanced over her shoulder not improved by the nasty, plastic whirring fan in front of her face.

"How was your journey down," Ros asked, quick to fill any pause.

"Pretty hot and boring. How was yours?"

"We had a couple of stop-overs including this delightful little village. Though when we were on the motorway it wasn't always easy to find places for Gavin Smee to do his injections. The heat makes him far worse, you know, we thought he might collapse at one point."

Leah had forgotten about the town clerk's poorly controlled diabetes. It was a further reminder that making her own way over rather than in the shared minibus with the others and avoiding all the hassles that came from travelling en masse was the right decision.

"What's your tipple," asked Ros, handing her the drinks menu.

"I'd like a limoncello, but I also want wine with my meal and can't go too mad because of the happy pills.... and the sleeping pills."

A brief pause.

Ros let out a quick shrill guffaw unsure if it was a joke but not wanting to dwell on anything she would consider to be 'a downer.'

Leah ordered a rum-free Pina colada which went well with the accompanying canapes and their salty hit of anchovy.

The pair exchanged nods of acknowledgment with other guests trickling through to restaurant before settling into their usual dynamic; Ros fussing, full of clichés and tedious commentary on everything around her, made tolerable by some inadvertent indiscretions and gossip that Leah extracted with ease

It meant that when the rest of the party arrived to join them – the mayor, his deputy, the town clerk and a work experience student, Matt, the attractive son of someone senior at the council, Leah had insights that gave her a much-needed feeling of control and superiority.

She now knew the mayor was divorcing his wife of 38 years (Jan Dunnett, his usual consort, not on the trip) after a two-year affair with his deputy Anne Sparks (on the trip). More interestingly, the council was millions in debt and perhaps not surprisingly eyebrows had been raised at the decision to continue with the swelling itinerary of town twinning events while the library was being replaced with a monthly book bus.

The party were shown to their table and Leah was pleased to be next to Dunnett with his easy, extrovert company and diagonally opposite the boy who would unwittingly provide some easy on the eye distraction if the evening dragged.

She noticed that the mayor's new love interest was sitting furthest away from him. She wondered if it was to deflect suspicion from their relationship or perhaps more grimly, as she eyed Dunnett's gut flopping over the waistband of his thin, white slacks, because they couldn't trust themselves to behave in close proximity.

"So, what's the big news in the Herald at the moment?" asked the mayor, helping himself to two chunks of bread and buttering both in the palm of his hand.

It was his standard and not altogether unreasonable way of starting most their conversations.

"It's the fifteenth anniversary of Tom Steadman's disappearance, so we'll do something on that. Speak to the parents, maybe his old teacher. You know the police have given us a new statement this time, basically saying the case is closed but it ..."

"Well that really should be the end of it, I mean, is anyone really that interested anymore?" interrupted Gavin Smee.

This was a rare deviation from his usual desperation to conform and agree with anyone around him.

"Gavin, it's the biggest news story ever in the town, an unsolved case, people still talk about," countered the mayor, on her behalf, spitting crumbs through a mouthful of bread.

"I feel dreadfully sorry for his family and that poor little boy, but I agree with Gavin it is a bit of a downer," added Ros. "I've lived in Maltham my whole life and I think people forget there is more to the town than a missing child. It's as if that's the only thing that's ever happened here."

Debate, for what it was, limped on during the terrine starter, while some measure of sobriety remained, along with discussing arrangements for meeting up with the French delegation tomorrow.

By the time the fish course arrived the conversation had risen in volume and lowered in calibre making way for gossip and shrieking that turned the heads of other bemused diners. For the time being, Tom Steadman was long forgotten.

4

France, July 2017

It was the 9 o'clock church chimes that finally pierced her deep medicated sleep. The last seven hours had been lost to oblivion but by dawn, Leah's mind was stirring with vivid, angsty dreams that included a sacking from some anonymous corporate behemoth and Ros's abuse of her Burberry handbag.

She finally awoke with a sedative-induced fog but at least having slept she was pragmatic about the trade-off. At their last session, her therapist had concluded that her intermittent insomnia was in fact therapy resistant. Leah wondered where the line was drawn between being therapy resistant and simply ineffective treatment, yet it confirmed that no amount of deep breathing or visualising forests could soothe her wired mind and body. When her whole being was racing with cortisol, she needed knocking out however artificial the means.

Her arm reached for the phone to order room service. The thought of joining the others downstairs in the petit salon for breakfast was unthinkable at this hour (9.20 am) when she had no sense of humour or patience for the kind of gregarious small talk expected in these situations.

She could picture them now chomping and guffawing, bearing the first blotches of heat rash, refreshed from a snore-ridden night and already at full volume - a seamless continuation from last night's banter. As her eyes surrendered to drowsiness, she thought how easy it must be to be like Dunkett able to negotiate life with a permanent grin and not too much analysis or introspection.

"Bon Matin, Mademoiselle, le petit déjeuner."

The high-pitched sing song voice jolted her, and she opened her eyes again. The patron knew not to wait for an answer or the indeed for the door to be opened. Well-drilled in this guest's idiosyncrasies, the tray was left outside ready for collection in her own time thereby avoiding any human interaction without having applied her make up.

Checking for sounds of imminent departures from the adjacent rooms, Leah opened the door slowly to find the usual wooden tray bearing pastries, a fruit salad, orange juice, tea and copy of Paris Match. Sat in bed prodding the teabag to extract some flavour she acquainted herself with the latest on Vanessa Paradis and the rest of the French glitterati that seemed to monopolise these pages year after year and which, as ever, was reliably absorbing.

The rich smack of melted chocolate from the choc au pain smothered the metallic after taste of her medication and the warmth of the mug in her hands provided a simple comfort. With the shutters still closed, everything at that moment was exactly how she liked it, dark, quiet and cosy, for the time being light, life and noise could wait.

* * *

"Look at you in your ripped jeans," said Ros to Leah. She had the bemused look of someone for whom such attire was not only solely for teenagers but totally unsuitable even on a jolly in southern France.

The pair were waiting in the hotel foyer for the rest of their group, ready to meet their French hosts and start the day's itinerary. Ros, who had never worn jeans in her life, was in the day version of her usual garb minus the scarf and broaches that only came out at night.

"It was such shame you didn't join us for breakfast. We were all having such a giggle, oh, such a giggle," she relayed face beaming at the memory.

"Vince couldn't remember the French word for jam which is actually coverture, and he kept saying...."

"Confiture," Leah corrected on autopilot her attention diverted to the work experience boy in his low-slung jeans and whose name she'd forgotten.

Ros also turned in his direction.

"Expect this is a bit early for you Matt. Don't youngsters normally like to sleep in until midday?"

Leah groaned inwardly at the use of the word youngster and at that moment her association with Ros as if the pair were peers which technically they were.

Matt replied: "Only with a hangover, I'm usually up much earlier to work out."

He had that easy well-bred confidence that could swot away dull people efficiently but with charm. He also had tired, sultry eyes and a winning coy smile, all in all that rather delicious fusion of innocence and knowingness exclusive to the very young and attractive just becoming aware of their currency.

The rest of the party followed shortly, and the main business began. It was a schedule that had barely changed in the last 15 years, with the usual focus on artisan factory workshop visits.

The group watched luxury calf-skin gloves being stitched at a nearby atelier before sampling the region's blue cheese with varying degrees of enthusiasm – ultimately pleasant but instantly forgettable little chunks of activity that filled sometime between café pitstops. The main event was to come.

* * *

The figure of Christ was held high on a plinth that bobbed and swayed as its six pallbearers dressed in long white robes negotiated uneven curbs and stray dogs.

Arms aloft and captured mid blessing, this Jesus had an almost regal air, swathed in decorative, richly coloured robes, flashes of deep crimson and gold that could be seen from any vantage point, bold and commanding against Saint Jean de Ruel's stony pastel streetscape.

Bunting and flags had been added to the already flower-strewn village resulting in mass of colour and clutter as people of all ages stood three-deep along the pavement and road clapping or with arms outstretched trying to touch the statue. While the tourists held their camera phones, the locals were too enrapt to dilute the moment through a lens. It was an all-consuming focus and enthusiasm which Leah found quite touching in its reverence, and why as the rest of her party remained at their vantage point outside the tabac struggling to grasp their host's commentary, she decided to follow Jesus with the locals.

Past the last few shops, cafes and swell of sweating, exuberant faces hanging out of windows and perched on various street furniture the procession entered its final stretch. A few flowers – modest stems plucked from the wild to more elaborate bouquets were thrown onto the plinth as it made the cautious ascent up the church steps and through a heavy, wooden door that opened on a cue by a priest inside.

And now amplified by multiple speakers along the main street, a samba beat shifted the vibe into a full-blown carnival; but as others danced, Leah entered the church, slapped by the cool, silent darkness as her senses adjusted. In a place where even the wind was hot, she appreciated the chill and settled on the back pew watching the Jesus figurine positioned at the foot of the alter with much deference and titivation that she knew would still have been applied regardless of any audience.

Flanked by eagle lecterns and impressive cascading blooms, the figurine seemed poised to deliver a sermon as the pallbearers retreated slowly down the aisle acknowledging Leah's presence with the restrained wordless nods that ecclesiastical settings dictate. A creak, a flash of daylight followed by a solemn thud, and she was alone.

The journalist didn't consider herself to be particularly religious, whatever that really meant anyway, but did believe in God with a faith and spirituality more easily stirred in these icon-heavy sanctuaries than the quasi-community centres back home. With the unstifled freedom of having the place to herself she began to explore, passing the various saint figures positioned high on the stone walls, identified by their respective symbols of roses, doves and daggers carved into their hands.

In the left corner hung a display of photographs of the town over the years revealing a rolling cast of inhabitants enjoying the same fetes and religious festivals against the same backdrops spanning both black and white and colour.

Now, at the altar, her eyes fell once again on the central Jesus figurine in front of a simple gold cross and stained-glass window of vivid blues and crimsons, emboldened by the searing sunlight.

The only other light came from a handful of long cream candles flicking amongst their shorter, extinguished counterparts. She put the smallest coin she had in the wooden collection box and took a candle from a pile underneath, lighting one whilst making the usual wish list of life improvements, peace for her troubled mind, success, validation, recognition, revenge. It was a lot to ask of this tiny, dancing flame but as always, she found some comfort in this small act and that was when she noticed it.

Propped between a small posy of black roses and the back of the candle rack was a small, creased photograph flecked with melted wax. A boy of around two or three perched on a young woman's knee, her face fixed indulgently on his slightly truculent expression, his dark eyes looking challengingly at the lens.

The journalist picked it up and read the scribbled note on the back which identified him as Jacque Renard – the young son of Monique Renard with the date: July 21st, 2000, and place: Saint Jean de Ruel and what translated as: "*He loved cats and trains*" – a sparce summation of a life presumably over before it had begun.

Peering closely in the poor light it was the familiarity of his stare that struck her. The intensity of the eyes, their green-brown colouring that could flit between olive and chocolate depending on the light and the angle, the hair that fell into a curly mop immune to attempts to be coaxed into a side parting.

Dressed in mustard corduroy trousers, a blue shirt and sleeveless knitted jumper, his chubby hands were clasped together resting on the small mound of his stomach, his bright red shoes dangling from his mother's knee.

She considered some of the telling descriptions of Tom Steadman from teachers and others that knew him in the aftermath of his disappearance; 'lively' 'challenging' 'strong-willed' - the usual diplomatic sweeteners to sugar coat what was obviously a difficult child, prone to playing up and having his own way.

It was the essence of the character in her hands now as she

picked off some wax in the corner of the image to reveal the rest of a ginger cat curled asleep. Taking it with her to the back pew, she reread the inscription before retrieving an image of Tom on her phone for comparison aware of a low thud of her heartbeat and sweep of adrenalin as she mulled over the repercussions of taking it with her.

Several minutes passed before the sound of the door made her draw breath and she grabbed a hymn book to cover her find. An elderly woman had entered. Aged and tiny, there were many of her sort in this village. This one had heels which nudged her frame to five foot and tapped rhythmically on the stone floor down the nave until she reached the front pew and knelt to pray. It was a protracted process and when her head disappeared from view the journalist returned her attention to the image, photographing it with her phone, its quiet click still stark in the silence.

She looked up, eyes returning to the gilt gaze of Jesus and his Mona Lisa-esque smile, her mind jostling between the improbable and her trusted instinct before drifting to the aftermath of Tom's disappearance. Recollections laced with odd detail came thick and fast; ripped bunting, a smudged footprint on a Union Jack Jubilee flag lying in the road, flying ants, tiny dots of torchlight from the search parties swallowed up in the black woodland and Carolyn Steadman's fluoride toothpaste smell.

And now familiar figures – old and new colleagues and members of the twinning party began to float away their usual settings to abstract worlds with only the lack of headrest and the pew's unforgiving rigidity stopping her from fully succumbing to the dregs of the sleeping pill still in her system.

Meanwhile, the building's other occupant began to stir, a small head materialising at the front leaving via a side entrance as the journalist looked at her watch to discover she had been here for over an hour. She returned the picture to the candle rack, absently stroking one of the black rose petals surprised to discover they were real.

* * *

A laboured internet search compromised by the hotel's erratic Wi-Fi told her the basics. Dubbed the 'Red Shoe Case' or the 'L'affaire of Petit Renard' depending on the media outlets, she learnt that the toddler had gone missing on July 21st, 2000, during the village's annual religious festival. No witnesses had come forward to report anything suspicious and with a propensity to wander off near the river and woods that backed his home, the theory was that the boy had either drowned or been attacked by wolves known to live there. The discovery of one of the boy's red T bar shoes in the vicinity had given credence to the theory.

Yet with no body found and tracking dogs unable to pick up his scent either near the river or deeper into the woods his mother, Monique, a single parent aged just 19 at the time who left the village a year later suspected foul play.

Rumours of an abduction lingered a theory stirred intermittently by false sightings. Police were convinced that if it was an abduction the toddler was likely to have known his kidnapper with various suspects including the usual black sheep relatives and family friends evaporating as fast as they appeared with no charges brought.

It seemed even his older cousins – aged eight and nine at the time - who had been queuing for drinks at a kiosk when the two year old wandered off - were subject to suspicion; rumours that there's had a been a malicious and deliberate neglect, an accusation slapped down by the family who had stressed how close they were, though admitted the boy was willful and sometimes hard to control.

Leah got to a quote from the grandmother in an interview with France 24 tv network a year on from the disappearance an elegant but drawn woman weighed down by events.

"I've replayed that morning again and again in my mind; him sitting at the dining table drinking his hot chocolate, eating a macaroon laughing his loud laugh at something his cousin had said. He was so excited to be going to the festival. I'll always have that regret I didn't go with him; because he'd be here now."

* * *

Aware she would be dining with members of the French twinning party at the hotel that evening Leah hoped to find out more of the hyper-local detail on the cold case. Yet, in reality, shoe-horning the affair into the group's meal was harder than anticipated.

Conversation that had started out as slightly stilted enquiries around their respective towns and customs due to the language barrier had made away for low brow, drink fueled banter amid the growing familiarity – broad jokes and anecdotes that couldn't be lost in translation.

High on the frisson of his not-so-secret lady friend and a receptive audience, Vince Dunkett led the high volume, easy laughs with no utterance complete without some sort of punchline however lame. Participants had reached that comfortable, undiscerning state where practically anything seemed hilarious.

Ordinarily, the journalist would have found this tiresome, but her own spirits had been lifted during this break, buoyed by her find in the church and the renewed focus it gave her inquisitive mind which always benefited from a distraction rather than introspection.

In the lull before the cheese course as the group temporarily dispersed for toilet and cigarette breaks course, she took the chance to probe the French mayor. Up to now, their interaction had been limited which explained why the small man with thick glasses looked surprised by her attention and the nature of the inquiries.

He reiterated much of what she had already read online, his only opinion on the matter was that he didn't believe the boy had been attacked by wolves because of the absence of remains and that this persistent theory had probably hindered the investigation.

Queries answered he was soon ready for an alternative distraction to draw this to a close, his face serious with a flicker of irritation over an unwelcome intrusion to the less complicated fun. Having covered the Tom Steadman case for so long, it was a reminder that for every person who wallowed in this kind of local folklore and seized the opportunity to elaborate, there were others who remained defensive, viewing such sagas as a stain on their local area's reputation which seemed to be the case here.

She could have felt deflated as she returned to her seat between Ros and Gavin but as the meal drew to an end these two irritants unwittingly morphed into amusing diversions while the warm, moreish wine and after dinner liquors had a mood lifting effect.

Opposite, sat 17-year-old Matt, free of the sweat, sunburn and food odours that seeped through the pores of some of the others, just the heavy-handed aftershave of adolescence which she quite liked for that reason along with his tendency to repeat some of her own turn of phrases and agree with her every utterance.

Afterwards she headed outside walking up the small gradient on her preferred right-hand side of the street, a lone evening stroll that reaffirmed the simple pleasure to be had when a breeze stirs after a stifling day in a place familiar but still fresh with possibility.

Shuttered shops smothered by the darkness made way for the tiny bars as the main hubs of activity as the distant buzz from the central café edged closer and more defined to reveal a packed courtyard, air thick with smoke and conversations.

She was debating whether to go in as a car drew level. The window lowered slowly to reveal the French deputy mayor, a small, non-descript woman, Leah had barely spoken to, dismissed with her usual haste as some mousy appendage to the more gregarious mayor. In common with many people she didn't take much notice of, closer inspection rendered some surprising details, mainly that she was a little younger and more attractive than her overall image conveyed from a quick glance.

She was leaning towards the open passenger window, a figurine of the singer Johnny Hallyday hung from the rear-view mirror and waved incongruously whenever contact was made.

"Mademoiselle, I wanted to speak to you. I heard you asking Monsieur Chalfont about Jacque Renard."

"Yes, do you know anything about it?"

"Look in the church, at the visitors' book, you will find something interesting, messages from someone saying they saw the boy being followed by a man along the Rue de Stade on July 21st in 2000. Of course, some people think it is a .... erm..."

She mumbled a few words to herself as her eyes darted around for inspiration.

"A sick joke?" offered Leah finally.

"Yes! A joke, but they have not stopped. They keep coming - more this month."

A flurry of fast French followed, some reference to the colour purple which the journalist couldn't properly grasp and now with the contribution imparted, the woman's window began to slowly rise.

"Does anyone know who is doing this?" asked Leah, crouched by the window.

"No. Nobody knows. Good evening." A small wave and the car drove off.

* * *

Up to now, Gavin Smee's laminated itinerary for the trip had served little more purpose than as a makeshift fly swotter. Leah purposely chose not to look at it too closely because there were times when she didn't want or need to know of a forthcoming activity that sounded dull or required a journey which would then entail repetitive conversations with the same people in a confined space. In her still fragile mental state, the prospect could loom heavy and lower her mood.

That morning, she did look and was relieved to discover the day had been earmarked as free time, meaning she could return to the church to follow up the deputy mayor's tip off. Ignoring the town clerk's suggestion to visit a nearby arboretum, she felt smug passing some of the group, subdued and nursing coffees in the Petit Salon, their puffy eyes betraying the effects of a cumulative hangover which meant each day now got off to an increasingly sluggish and delayed start.

At the church which she had to herself, she found the current visitors' book and a pile of older editions on the shelf of a small bookcase that also stored surplus candles and more mysteriously bottles of tea tree oil.

Taking all six books to what had become her usual position at the far end of the back pew, she flicked through pages thick with illegible scrawls and gushing puff from tourists praising the well-kept 'facility' as if it was a tearoom. As indicated by the deputy mayor, the references to Jacque Renard's abduction were mostly written in July and September, and she discovered, easily identifiable by the use of a fountain pen with deep purple ink which looked bold and stylish amongst the faded blue and black biro.

The first message appeared in July 2001 and translated as:

"A tall, white man in his 30s followed the missing boy Jacque Renard down the Rue de Stade during the village religious festival on July 21st, 2000. I saw him. No one else did. The man did not see me."

The second written in September of the same year, repeated much of the previous entry with a lament that they should have done something but couldn't. This had prompted a flurry of riled responses, with references to fiction and lies, heavy with exclamation marks applied with a pen pressure that indented the next few pages.

The journalist photographed all of the messages before replacing the books. She returned when she could usually follow a similar routine of checking the photograph which remained in its usual place on the candle rack and noting the addition of fresh flowers next to it.

"What is the obsession with that place?" Ros enquired one morning in the petit salon, looking up from her word search.

"Didn't have *you* down as a paid-up member of the god squad."

Leah noted the faintly amused smirk as the woman carefully circled the name of tv host and then went over it again with a pink highlighter, her tongue lolling in concentration. The journalist was curious as to what Ros's questionable logic made her such an unlikely candidate but anticipating the drivel that would come back, chose not to pursue it.

"Not convinced of a higher power yourself then Ros?"

The blank face suggested not.

"Leah, when we're alive, we're alive and when we're dead, we're dead. As far as I'm concerned, the only things in the sky are the birds and clouds and not a man with a beard."

She gave a little shake of the head, eyes still fixed on her wordsearch.

"Well, you seem very convinced," said Leah. "Anyway, I'll leave you to it.

"Oh, this thing," The press officer waved the book dismissively. "It fills twenty minutes."

As Leah remembered from their dealings the first-time round, Ros often described her activities and reading matter in this way. Whether it was the Enid Blyton books from her childhood she regularly re-read or her adult colouring book the aim was to imply it was all a rare deviation from her usual more heavyweight intellectual pursuits, which of course it wasn't.

5

Jean de Ruel, France, July 2017

Tobacco and expensive scent competed in the late afternoon breeze, a sweet, oaky alchemy that wafted around *Le Chat Noir*'s elegant courtyard.

People-watching from this central café had been a simple ritual of Leah's week in Jean de Ruel but the prospect of tomorrow's return was already encroaching into an otherwise idyllic scenario and affecting her mood. She ordered an Americano and returned the glance of an attractive man seated nearby with his wife feeling open to a bit of capricious distraction.

"Voila Mademoiselle," said the waiter, arriving with the coffee and jug of water she always ordered.

She bit into the accompanying pink macaroon while scanning a two-day old copy of The Times to read news she hadn't missed while in this particularly languid bubble.

"Somebody's all on their tod aren't they"?

Gavin Smee had appeared from nowhere with his usual taut smile that never reached his eyes.

She looked up reluctantly.

Of indeterminate age, with his height, broad shoulders and even features he should have had some sort of physical appeal, but the reality was entirely sexless. Perhaps it was an existence defined by pandering to the egos of more powerful men at the council or that impenetrable bland efficiency that climaxed around those who in his eyes mattered the most or dated jeans sitting to high on the ankle. There was much to choose from.

"Are the others inside?" he asked hopefully.

"Nope just me; they've probably returned to the hotel by now."

A flicker of disappointment but he felt compelled to stay out of professional duty and persist with meaningless, distracted small talk while texting his council colleagues.

"Standing in the Black Cat café courtyard with Leah. Where are you. Exclamation mark."

Each word and punctuation were voiced slowly with precision while his manicured fingers went into overdrive.

Did it really matter she thought, they'd be having dinner together in about an hour.

"Anything urgent Gavin"?

"Oh no, nothing important at all."

Or nothing he'd choose to share with her she thought.

He continued texting while firing anodyne questions and comments her way as if he obliged to keep her amused: Had she enjoyed the week? Was she looking forward to getting back? The weather had been especially hot this year, hadn't it? She had noticed before how their interaction tended to follow the tedious template of the one she had with her beauty therapist who often repeated the same questions during each appointment because she never listened to the answers.

And now he was scanning the surrounding streets in the hope of transferring his attentions to one of the others. She drank her coffee and studied him with utter contempt and considered if there anything more exasperating than being found dull and unworthy by a loser like Gavin Smee.

"Gavin, you look very tired," she said finally seizing the initiative. "Are your blood sugar levels ok? Perhaps you need to go back and rest for a bit."

She surprised herself with the convincing show of sincerity.

"Actually, I'm not feeling too good. It's the heat really, I should get a soft drink and sit down for a bit."

Leah's eyes went skyward. She now faced the prospect of him joining her and having one of his hypo episodes with only her for assistance. God, how she resented all this. She wanted to sit here alone with her thoughts and plans. If Ros had been present, she would be genuinely concerned and take over any the responsibility fussing around and fetching whatever he needed. Leah, however, was a very different proposition and remained seated observing with mild curiosity the town clerk's hesitant shuffle towards the café like a geriatric as he tried to locate something in his man bag.

If he collapsed inside, the bartender would be there to take charge, she reasoned, taking another sip of water and meeting the eyes of her admirer at the nearby table.

Gavin eventually returned with a can of limeade clutching the back of the seat to steady himself before sitting slowly. Trembly hands struggled with the ring pull which he eventually released and gulped the contents quickly.

For once, his tiresome commentary had ceased as he stared ahead with a vacant look. The pair sat in silence for a few minutes with Leah strangely intrigued to see this most clinical of characters in a more compromised and vulnerable state, surrendering to the power of his condition he couldn't control, thinking it was the only time she had ever found him interesting. She flicked a sugar sachet towards him, but he shook his head and raised the can slightly to indicate the drink was enough. A few more slips followed by some rapid blinks and a more familiar persona began to return from wherever it had been.

As he came around, she remembered the one question she had actually wanted to ask him.

"Gavin you were here on the twinning trip in 2000 weren't you"?

"Of course, why do you ask?"

"You don't remember a young boy disappearing from the village festival in that year do you"?

A long pause.

"Do I remember a young boy disappearing from the village festival," he repeated her question slowly with a hint of condescending bemusement as if indulging a particularly stupid child.

"No, I don't think I do Leah."

"A toddler called Jacque Renard, rumoured to have wandered off possibly drowned or attacked by the wolves in the Bois de Foret - though his mother suspected an abduction."

"Eaten by wolves.... god how awful, all sounds a bit Grimm's Fairy-tale, no I don't remember that at all," he wasn't really very interested, an apathy that extended to most things beyond his town council bubble and duties and as he got up quickly it sparked another wave of dizziness.

A brief pause as he steadied himself.

"Right now, I'm feeling a bit better, so I think I'll head back and get a shower. See you shortly. Sorry about all that palaver."

It was his usual sign off after one of his episodes had run his course.

"Ok, see you at dinner."

She watched him make his way down the street not looking ok at all.

* * *

The final five course meal of the visit had slipped down nicely. As she stood on her balcony releasing the pressure on her tightening trouser zip and mentally bidding goodbye to a familiar scene for another year, she realised she would miss this.

For the first time though she was looking at it all through a different lens as her eyes fell on the model wolves on the riverbank and she realised the scene before her was no longer an untainted idyll.

6

Maltham, August, England 2017

In a town where the wealth was split between old and new money, David and Carolyn Steadman occupied the former, flashier camp; neighbours to a popstar 'name' from the 80s in one of the substantial piles overlooking a famous golf course.

It was a set up that suited Carolyn well. Her East End roots may have imparted a certain savviness but there was no real intellect or professional ambitions; and as the fragrant other half of her self-made alpha husband neither had been required.

Occasional stints doing admin at David's agency remained her only (heavily resented) foray in the workplace despite the lifestyle it afforded and the rarity of request. No, her raison d'etre was to run her big house and enjoy the long summer socials at the couple's Spanish villa and the unspoken kudos that came from being the most photogenic of her peers.

In the immediate aftermath, devoid of her self-appointed purpose, the vacuity of her existence had been heavily exposed. A missing child had dampened a social scene that wanted little more than uncomplicated drink-fuelled euphoria from its participants. The bitch and brag sessions that once bookended her daily workouts at the health club were never quite the same again which is why a gym had been installed in their home so she could continue her strict routine mostly alone with her personal trainer.

Meanwhile, visitors to the house had remained an eclectic and often unwelcome bunch; police of varying capabilities and press from tabloid journalists to editors of obscure crime blogs. Then there were those who had simply enjoyed wallowing in the drama under the guise of concern, including the woman who had quickly ingratiated herself into Carolyn's life and had been caught loitering outside the couple's property in the early hours.

For the Maltham Herald, the Steadman's stalker was just another spin off in a narrative that never stopped giving. The culprit, a teaching assistant at Tom's school, was cautioned by police and outed in the paper to much drama and judgement, a saga that had taken care of the front page for the last three weeks and incurred a record number of reader's letters all of which from the Herald's perspective had been welcome and timely during the traditionally slow news month of August.

Now with the fifteenth anniversary of Tom's disappearance looming and the police's decision to put the investigation on hold once again, Leah's Dictaphone sat expectantly on a glass coffee table between herself and Carolyn.

The pair were making stilted small talk on opposite blush pink couches waiting for David to join them. The room was as stylish and sterile as Leah remembered as was Carolyn with her olive colouring, long dark hair and heart-shaped face, a very conventional prettiness bolstered further by a teenage-lean body well into forties.

The lack of body fat had gone against her in the rawest,

tearstained aftermath where shock and worry were etched deeply on a face with no cushioning. Yet heated anguish had transitioned to numb acceptance. Life had rumbled on, and she was too rich and image conscious to surrender to the physical deterioration that can afflict those in similar circumstances. With subtle cosmetic interventions and less alcohol consumption than before her beauty was almost restored.

"So sorry guys, I got held up in the office."

Resigned to their lack of commonality and mutual indifference, both women were relieved to see him and be rescued from their stiff small talk. He and Leah shook hands. She had always preferred him of the two, he was warmer, more open and had remained remarkably resilient in spite of events. She noticed that he had acquired the slightest paunch, and his hair had thinned but neither had really dented his appeal rooted in success and conventional good looks.

"We've just taken on a new account manager, so I'm having to hand hold a bit at the moment, until she gets used to everything," he said sitting next to his wife, legs apart, leaning back with a relaxed confidence.

Leah caught the quickest look of rebuke from Carolyn and was intrigued as to implications of this apparent faux pas.

"No worries," said the journalist as she took a slug of disappointing coffee. She liked it strong with a kick while Carolyn had served up some insipid decaffeinated affair that was more like a hot milkshake.

"So, I thought we could start perhaps with your thoughts on the 15th anniversary of your son's disappearance, four years on from the police's decision to close investigation."

"It's a marker of those lost years," said Carolyn crossing her legs. "David and me have a nephew who is now 17 – Tom's cousin so you're reminded what he could be like now because in many ways he's frozen in time as a little schoolboy."

"And is there still hope?"

"It was very disappointing when the investigation was closed but of course it doesn't mean *we're* going to give up on finding Tom," said David pointedly. "There's still no evidence to suggest he's no longer with us and until that changes we'll always have hope."

Leah's long finger edged the Dictaphone closer to the target.

"You think the police could and *should* still be doing more then because there was some criticism about the costs involved?"

"Well, yes I suppose so." said David,

"Yes and no," said Carolyn, an indecisive answer delivered in a very decisive tone.

She threw up a pointed manicured finger towards her husband to indicate she was taking over and he was to stop talking.

"It's disappointing in some ways, but we appreciate that there isn't a bottomless pit of resources, and we also know that the door isn't closed. There's every chance that new leads will keep coming and we've been assured that when they do the police will give them their full attention."

It was all very much her Modus Operandi quashing any sniff of meatier opinion with something script-reading generic. This denial of anything more meaningful, that properly conveyed or reflected the torment that still must be raging meant the kind of killer quote that would have elevated Leah's copy was routinely denied which irritated the journalist immensely. She knew has she took another sip of tepid coffee that she would have to put some effort in to make it a strong read and as usual, she really didn't have the energy.

It was a familiar pattern. Even in the immediate aftermath when victims are at their most vulnerable, the woman had been steely enough to steer questions in her preferred direction never getting drawn on the more personal and emotive. For Leah, this lack of compliance and an unspoken power struggle that existed between them was the reason she disliked her, not to a huge degree but enough not to feel any great empathy, which was odd given the context of their dealings.

"All I can do is focus on being productive in my own way with these sorts of projects," Carolyn continued as a hardback book materialised from a side table and was handed to Leah.

Entitled *My Son Tom: A Mother's Story*, the journalist's first impressions were that it seemed a curious take on the usual missing person memoirs, more of a plush coffee table tome. Leah flicked through it, her internal critic taking in the sparse, cliché-ridden text which had still required the services of a ghost writer; little more than musings and anecdotes with very little reference to the investigation.

All was improved slightly by a good mix of images of the family – showing a steady stream of holidays that accounted for the couple's permanent tans spanning their Spanish villa, skiing in Morzine and dune buggy rides in the Dubai desert. In others Tom hugged his pets, posed in his prep school uniform and leaned against different 4x4s.

"We just wanted people to get more of a sense of what Tom is like really," Carolyn added filling the silence. "Beyond the same image that's always in the papers."

Leah nodded compliantly but struggled to pass any favourable comment thinking there was little insight here.

She pretended to write something in her Moleskin notebook to buy some time while she thought of another question. It was always important to her that her questions appeared to flow seamlessly without any hint that she'd run out of ideas even when she was struggling as was the case here.

Yet she knew from experience that any attempt to extract more substance was largely in vain. Carolyn was no intellectual heavy weight, but she had a controlling, careful efficiency that tended to dictate the scenario and have the last word, which meant this new book would have to provide the main story angle for now however flimsy.

The journalist took another sip of weak coffee. The edge of the photo showing Jacque Renard's chubby hand was just visible in the note holder of her book prompting her final question which she delayed until the three were stood in the hallway and Carolyn had opened the front door.

"I'm surprised you didn't include any pictures of Tom as a baby."

"Sorry?" said Carolyn.

"In your new book. I don't remember seeing any in there."

"We just chose the ones we liked best really, and I think you get more of a sense of Tom's character when he was a little older," she said quite blankly.

Leah was relieved to return to the mess and familiarity of her VW. The ignition activated a loud blast of Nina Simone on the CD player as she pulled out of their gravel drive monitored by Carolyn from the front room window.

7

Maltham, England, August 2017

"I was looking over my notes going back to some of our earliest sessions and what struck me the most is how often you use the word 'offended'."

The comment hung expectantly in the air as Leah mulled over the implications.

It was a recurring theme in therapy, her inquisitive mind over-thinking lines of questioning and the specifics of their motivation rather than reacting instinctively as was encouraged. It meant that for much of their sessions in the cramped airless room next to the eating disorder clinic and an M&S hospital shop a sort of mutual analysis was taking place. Questions would be posed, and chains of thought would unravel and digress into broader, psychoanalysis in a way that did not happen with Ali Nixon's other clients.

Leah never looked forward to the prospect of picking over the minutiae of her current existence with its thwarted professional ambitions and frustrations no nearer to resolution but recognised the value of unravelling the knots of her troubled mind to a relative stranger.

While efforts to address her sleep disorder been put on hold on account of them not working, the therapist had agreed that their sessions should continue with more general talking therapy to deal with her anxiety and anger issues. Even in her cynical state, Leah appreciated the woman's effort and ability to remain totally transfixed however repetitious or self-indulgent the musings.

"Well, I suppose I do feel offended by all sorts of people," she offered eventually. "And it seems to happen all the time; in shops, restaurants, the office, particularly the office."

She paused, mentally trawling through years of hassle and aggravations, falling outs, bad atmospheres, revenge, and confrontation and yes, how she routinely felt very offended.

"But I've always been extremely sensitive and paranoid, at times, so perhaps it's not that surprising."

"Interesting that you use the word paranoid." Ali said.

"Is it?"

"Yes, because it's a rather negative and judgemental term that suggests you feel like you're overreacting to things when that may not necessarily be the case."

She had removed her glasses that sat on her head, releasing a glossy, chestnut fringe and layers that fell around the face.

"Though what I was getting at more was the choice of word 'offended'".

"Oh, right."

"It's quite clinical and unemotional, isn't it? I mean you don't just say you're upset, angry or pissed off, even – just offended."

Again, her patient wrestled with the lingual significance, though presumed it conveyed some emotionally detachment.

Ali filled the pause.

"I think you present this very tough girl image that is quite hard to break through, but I can see that there have been changes over the last two months. I can see a warmer more open side and some huge progress from the person that was sat in front of me at the beginning."

Though Leah wasn't entirely convinced she granted her a weak smile; a gesture seized with a wide-grinned enthusiasm by the therapist as if coaxing a reluctant toddler to say it's first word. She sometimes wondered if she was meant to cry in these sessions or if sometimes it would be easier if she did.

She had surmised early on that any self-criticism wasn't de rigour within these particular four walls. Yet this blameless positivity did at times jar with here more no-nonsense pragmatism that recognised her own judgement could be skewed and that very often she did look for the worst in people and situations.

She was also aware of how intolerant she had become and how she was irritated by pretty much everyone she encountered; from the bloody woman in the health shop earlier parroting inquiries about a reward card to some poor sop who dared to call her office landline with what they believed constituted a news story.

In short, these mild irritants that others would shrug off with a smile, for her took on disproportionate level of angst and exasperation. Was there anything so wrong in recognising that her behaviour and attitude could at times, just simply be bad, no excuses. It was ironic that the one place she felt more honest and self-critical was an environment where the most excuses were made.

"Ok," said Ali slowly and cautiously as if breaking bad news.

"We are coming to the end of the hour, but I want to briefly revisit what you mentioned last week when you discovered your former boss' offensive email and what he had been saying about you - I could see that there was still a lot of emotion there that hasn't be addressed yet."

The Missing Boy 49

Now this was a genuinely interesting remark. She thought she'd disguised it and had been surprised herself by how breathless she had become when relaying the story, an unease she'd tried to disguise by taking more sips of water.

"It was the shock of it, those words in black and white. I knew that I'd irritated him but had no idea there was so much resentment. What I was being called and the fact I was being laughed about by a team of people and knowing that at moment I had to leave and could never work there again."

"And this was your dream job, wasn't it? The national newspaper"?

"Yes."

"But we also know that these people were talking rubbish, that it is evidently clear to any intelligent person that you're not fat and you're not a bitch."

Leah thought briefly about contesting the latter but remained silent.

Her therapist pressed on: "What I really admire about you is that you own you're issues and personal challenges. You admit that there was some provocation on your part, that there were things you did in that office that weren't professional but at the end of the day no one deserves to be spoken about like that, and you've actually been very strong in getting on with your life and not letting this business defeat you."

But Ali's words intended as a concluding pep talk faded as the previous night's activity filled Leah's mind; how she had waited until dark to throw her used sanitary towel into the garden of the house that backed onto hers. It belonged to a family she didn't know but couldn't stand because of their hot tub, trampoline and barbeques and recently erected bar in the garden used for parties attended by their equally loud friends and screaming kids. She had planned to tell her this because she knew this wasn't entirely normal behaviour and was genuinely curious as to what kind of excuse Ali would find.

But she also knew proceedings were ending and as always Ali was trying to wind things up on a more optimistic note that would signify another step on a supposedly ever-rising arc of progress and improvement.

This revelation would be an unwelcome fly in the ointment, a downer to coin one of Ros's regular soundbites. Her therapist would respond carefully with the more inquisitive expression she adopted when addressing murkier territory but ultimately, there would be disappointment. Leah realised in this rare moment of indecision that she didn't like disappointing Ali with her belief and enthusiasm and good hair.

To some extent this meant that it was still an edited version of herself that was being assessed and analysed, a theme that was consistent with all her bouts of therapy over the years which made it all a little pointless.

* * *

Afterwards, with the session replaying on her mind as it often did, she headed to the town's police station. Here, she would meet Nicola Prescott, a former Herald reporter and now police press officer to go through the monthly crime round up committed by the great and good of Maltham.

This roll call of Waitrose shoplifting charges and anti-social behaviour confined to the pocket of a single, troubled estate that blotted the town's otherwise sanitised appearance was delivered by a woman who had lived and worked here for too long. It meant she had acquired an excessive level of interest in the minutiae of her local community usually the preserve of older people struggling to fill their time in retirement. This manifested itself in a compulsion to add erroneous detail to the reports either about the perpetrator, victim, or crime site however tenuous and absurd.

"She was the one who kept laughing during her facials," she'd report gravely on the woman caught jumping a red light on the school run.

"Proper cracking up apparently, the girl in the salon told me, they had to stop the treatment and now they won't see her at all. But that's the thing, how can anyone massage a face that's moving about like?"

or ....

"She'd got hold of a fluorescent dog coat for her spaniel to pass it off as one of those emotional support dogs – got free entry to everything going – exhibitions, concerts.... priority seats on public transport. People like that spoil it for others that really need to use these dogs to get around; it's just not on, is it?"

Leah didn't answer. She would sit in the cramped meeting room struggling to stay alert enough to extract the details that mattered while letting the rest drift over her, a balance that wasn't always easy in her usual medicated haze.

When things became especially tedious, her mind wandered to her own indiscretions at the supermarket self-service check out till; where the odd £20 jar of Manuka honey or specialist olive oil she fancied but didn't want to pay for would bypass the scanner and how as a result she ran the risk of featuring on this sorry list she reported on.

The crime round up didn't even need to be carried out in person. Email would have sufficed, but it was an arrangement her editor wanted to continue under the guise of building community relations. Leah had been in no rush to change it either because it got her out of the office and an opportunity, she would fully exploit with a detour to the coffee shop and discreet mooch around the shops on the other side of town that would fill another half an hour.

Maltham being Maltham, where people's disposable income tended to exceed their style credentials it meant mainly rip off boutiques with names like Mia and Lemon and Chloe Loves Cupcakes, run by loud, fake women in espadrille wedges selling £300 jeans

In a misguided attempt to bond, or more accurately flog some wisp of polyester for £90 they would start up a conversation about Prosecco or their kids usually before adding helpfully that other sizes (i.e. larger than size 8) were available. It was the kind of drivel that confirmed that there was probably no one she related to less than these sort of women despite the probably similar age and she always left without spending, deriving some satisfaction from wasting their time as well as own.

Two or more hours would pass during these mid-weeks skives so that by the time she returned to her desk she felt compelled to explain it away with some comment about the rise in the crime that had delayed her at the station.

It was a pitiful charade, that she was embarrassed to be reduced to doing and it usually prompted a raised eyebrow from the editor's secretary who would shuffle in her seat, face fixed on her screen struggling not to let rip with her opinions,

At today's briefing though, Leah had a greater sense of purpose. The picture of Jacque Renard in her notebook finally needed to be shared and while Nicola herself was pointless, she could at least suggest the best contact to share new information with regarding the Tom Steadman case.

She waited until the end of the crime list and the usual final item on unresolved dog fouling on the recreation ground that came up every week before producing the image.

"Remind you of anyone?" Leah asked, her heart rate quickening as she looked at it properly for the first time that week handing it to the press officer with a flourish.

Nicola scanned it her face blank.

"You'll have to help me out - who is this"?

"He's a boy that went missing in France during a festival in 2000 called Jacque Renard, but doesn't he look familiar to you? I think there's a strong resemblance to Tom Steadman. What do you reckon"?

"Tom Steadman." The press officer repeated the name slowly as the implications sunk in.

"Bloody hell Leah, you've spent too long reporting on that saga; you know they've closed the case – some time ago from what I can remember."

"Of course, I do," she snapped huffily instantly regretting showing her image.

"Where did you get this from?" She waved the image to one side with a flick of the wrist, which in Leah's eyes, showed insufficient respect and offended her.

"In a church in Saint Jean De Ruel during the council twinning visit the other week. But not only do the boys look very similar, they've gone missing from twinned towns do you not think that's a bit of an odd coincidence?"

"Well, I wouldn't say they look *that* similar. Are you actually saying you think it's the same kid?"

Exasperation was building inside of Leah as she watched with tired eyes what had consumed and invigorated her for the last week now being swotted away like a fly.

"I'm trying to think what Tom Steadman looks like ...." the press officer continued, her face fixed in an unflattering grimace, discoloured, uneven teeth on show as she tried to recall.

Leah had had enough.

"Well, if you can't even remember what he looks like, then you're not really able to judge if this one looks like him or not," she said whipping the image from her hand.

"Maybe not, I'm clearly not as close to the whole affair as you obviously are," said Nicola, prickling at the journalist's tone.

"And why is that, Nicola? It's only the biggest crime story to ever come out of this town – and there might just be a very significant update but why concern yourself with anything like this when you discuss dog shit for the sixth week in a row."

Her heart was racing now; it was technically her first work-related altercation since she returned, and that familiar loss of control and professionalism began to seep in with all its usual tedious consequences playing out in her mind. But nothing could stop it.

"In fact, all you really needed to say was that you weren't sure and left it there, rather than dismissing what is actually a very credible connection just so you can get on with your online shopping."

The press officer's expression began to switch from defensive to a more bemused pity which only made it worse as she put down the clipboard, crossed her legs and leaned in.

"Leah are you ok? I know that things have been a bit difficult, I'd heard that there was some sort of issue in London...."

"It's nothing to do with that, any of that," snapped the journalist putting the image in the sleeve of her notebook and I'd rather you didn't patronise me or comment on things you know nothing about."

Leah was irritated but mainly with herself. None of this needed to have happened. Why had she even bothered sharing this with Nicola in the first place, the woman was a failed journalist who had switched to press office work for more regular hours at the request of her tedious childhood sweetheart. With her bad teeth and wardrobe - today, she was even wearing a jumper with an attached shirt collar to give the impression of a separate shirt worn underneath. Her opinion counted for nothing.

Leah gathered her bag and notebook and stood up.

"Anyway, I need to get in touch with one of the forensic

experts, one of the age progression artists who created the images of Tom at 10 and 15, they could do the same with this one for comparison."

Nicola had just removed a hot chocolate sachet from her handbag and was now standing up.

"Well, good luck with that but the case is closed isn't it", she repeated adopting the blank efficiency of someone trying to draw things to a close and extract herself from the situation and company as quickly as possible.

"Yes, it's on hold, but obviously if things come up, they'll be looked at won't they, they won't just be ignored."

The pair parted awkwardly, Leah already going through the tedious follow emails that would need to be sent to smooth things over. A big proviso of her employment here – which she'd secured without a vacancy and a more generous salary than the rest of the team was to be on her best behaviour; in the words of her editor hoping for an easy run up to retirement: NO MORE BLOODY DRAMA.

8

London, England 2000

"The thing is I don't want a kid that's already nine or 10 with a difficult past, I don't want a project from a children's home or China, I wanna be a mum, not a social worker, a normal mum with a regular baby like other people, easy, uncomplicated. Why is that so difficult?".

The therapist nodded carefully, observing the wired presence in front her, the young woman, thin and small on the chair, legs double crossed, a liberal douse of CK One failing to mask the faint scent of cigarette and fluoride.

Acquired in Mauritius, Carol Steadman had the healthy, even colour of an authentic tan yet today her make up sat a little heavy on her drawn, tired face. The overall effect muted her usual beauty, while a gaping waistband on her leggings brought focus to a shrinking frame rather than toned midriff.

The therapist asked: "Do you feel that this is the only option open to you now?".

"Well, the IVF's going nowhere and costing a fortune, I

dunno..." Carolyn trailed off looking ahead wearily. "Actually, it's not the money it's the eggs.... Last Friday, the woman from the clinic phoned to say that the four eggs they'd collected from me, you know to be transferred to my uterus had stopped growing. Just stopped growing. So that was that. Terrific."

She let out a little scornful laugh with a shake of the head.

"That must have been very difficult Carolyn."

Carolyn agreed.

"Perhaps the adoption people think that you and your husband would be well-equipped to cope with a more challenging placement, that you may have a lot to offer a child with a troubled past."

She watched Carolyn shrug her shoulders unconvinced but was well-used to her optimistic prompts being batted away.

"Actually, I reckon it's more to do with my husband's assault conviction than anything, you know, beggars can't be choosers and all that – 'let's give them a difficult one'."

"I'm sure that's not the case at all."

Silence.

"Would you like to talk about your husband's assault conviction"?

No, she wouldn't. Trawling through the particulars of another problem, another black mark and blemish that couldn't be changed, just to be met with well-meaning nods what was the point.

She squeezed her fists tight against her thighs, freshly manicured nailing digging hard into the palms inducing the faintest sting of pain. Nowhere did her fragile emotional state ebb and flow more acutely than in these intense, claustrophobic sessions. Free of the constant stimulus she relied on to make life bearable, here, time hung oppressively discussing issues that would otherwise be buried or left to erupt sporadically during drunken fights with her husband.

She continued: "And this woman from the agency kept talking about the unique demands of adoption and how these kids can be this and that and make such progress and it's all very rewarding and do you know what I was really thinking?

The therapist shook her head.

"That it feels like a sales pitch, and I just don't wanna know really."

She took a bottle of water from her gym bag, for something to do rather than thirst and to have a break from talking. Her hand trembled a little as she drank, betraying a vulnerability at odds with the soulless, anodyne delivery. After another sip she replaced the lid very slowly, screwing it tight and tighter before staring at the floor, momentarily so absorbed in her melancholy and frustrations and some random stain on the thin carpet, it was as if she forgot where she was and that there was someone else in the room.

Finally, the therapist tipped her head to one side, making a few small, silent nods in a bid to rouse her.

"And then I was thinking that I don't even know what the kid looks like. There's been no photos nothing, so I'm already suspicious, like, what exactly are they hiding and holding back? You know it was all about interrogating me, wanting to know every single thing about my bloody life, but what if I didn't like the child? What if it didn't look right anyway? It would all be for nothing."

"Tell me what you mean by 'looking right' Carolyn?"

"Attractive," she replied absently eyeing the pack of Marlborough lights in her gym bag as her therapist made notes with a carefully neutral expression.

"Why do you think that is so important to you?"

Her client looked up betraying a certain incredulity over the need for the question.

Eventually she said: "Well isn't that what everyone wants. I mean, given the choice, who would want an unattractive child? Ideally, I want a pretty girl that looks like it's my kid, y'know, dark eyes and hair, like it came out of my womb, that's important, it has to be plausible; I've always had this image in my head of what my family would be like and it's very difficult to compromise."

She got out a tube of her hand cream and dispensed a blob in both palms before rubbing them together fast and furiously for some time.

"Nice smell," she said to herself absently replacing the lid and dropping it in her bag.

The therapist said: "I think you're a person who likes to be in control and is used to perfection in many aspects of your life which has made this struggle to start a family especially painful for you and understandably so and no one is judging you for it."

Why had she even said that? It was precisely the kind of comment that did make Carolyn feel judged, delivered by someone better educated and better spoken, who no doubt had her own large brood of biological children and saw the woman sat in front of her as vain, stupid and shallow.

She was now looking at her therapist's bowed head as she made notes, hair in need of a wash and some highlights she thought. Beyond thinking that she needed to lose weight, Carolyn had never given the woman any thought whatsoever, an indifference that manifested in her calling her Cathy instead of Katy.

In common with the coterie of people who flitted in and out her life for an hour or so each week, from the masseuse to the gardener she was simply another anonymous individual there to serve a function. For the first time though, Carolyn considered the woman's life beyond these four walls.

"Do you have children?

"Yes, I have four – three boys and a girl."

Hence the waistline she thought to herself.

"I'm just interested in your motivation with all of this," the therapist continued, keen to deflect the focus.

"And I'd like to pick up on something else. I know from previous sessions, that when you talk about many aspects of your life you mention your husband a lot; he seems a big influence in many ways, my impression is that he is a big character. Yet in relation to your struggle to start a family, you barely mention him. It's almost as if he isn't part of this process. I wondered if that was something you want to discuss further?"

"Well, I suppose it's because I'm the one that can't have kids and it's not even like it's just one of those things like fate; I've done it to myself; It's my fault."

"How do you mean Carolyn?"

"I've made myself infertile with my eating disorder and even though it's had this effect I still can't stop even now, you know …. it's who I am, part of me and my routine."

"You can't stop your bulimia?"

"Yeah, so I feel it's my problem to sort out. Anyway, David is very wrapped up in his business, it's his life, so he's focused on that – he wants me to be happy and have what I want but he's less …. I dunno…."

"Emotionally invested?"

"Yeah."

"I think it's important that you try not to see this as something that is your fault and that only you can fix. This situation isn't about blaming yourself or anyone else and things are really far from helpless there are options open to you…."

But now as always, at around this time in the session when her attention span finally imploded the words had become background noise, faintly audible but redundant as Carolyn nodded flatly on cue while drifting to her own preferred solution. It was a fantasy that had formed as they so often do – to address the limitations and inadequacies of real life, honed while staying at the various interchangeable luxury resorts she visited every year where she had even more time on her hands than usual.

Here, somewhere hot and expensive, with her mind primed on the target, she would see opportunity everywhere during languid poolside days, where parents distracted by new friends, cocktails and complacency with the growing familiarity of their surroundings took risks and short cuts over child supervision.

On jaunts beyond the hotel complex, she would see an abundance of poor and photogenic local children some aged around three or four roaming freely without any sign of an adult. It was opportunity compounded by the simple virtue of being somewhere else. In her troubled mind, the language barrier, anonymity and her assumption that the local authorities would be less efficient all meant less risk and conspired to make the unthinkable a vague possibility.

"Sorry Carolyn, I was saying that the situation is no one's fault," prompted the therapist.

"Pardon?"

"About your difficulties with starting a family."

"Isn't it? I suppose in some ways we're both to blame."

She took a deep sigh, bored now; bored of talking. To her, the session had reached a natural conclusion even though it was flat and unsatisfactory with her torment no closer to any resolution as she gathered her handbag.

"Ok Carolyn, well we'll leave it there for today and I will see you next week."

"Yeah, ok."

The young woman got up, momentarily floored by a wave of dizziness that caused her to hold the chair for support.

"Oh, actually Cathy you won't. Sorry, I was going to say earlier, but me and my husband are moving house very soon and the next couple of weeks are going to be mad busy getting everything in order, so I think this will be the last session."

"Oh, that it is a shame Carolyn, are you completely sure? It's always better to finish the full course of sessions and we've made good progress."

"Yeah, I know, but I can't really see a way round it. It's been helpful though," she lied.

Her therapist sensed the futility of any more persuasion in the way she knew it wasn't worth correcting her whenever she called her Cathy. As a result, she settled for polite small talk about the house move to the town of Maltham and a stilted goodbye watching the woman retreat down the corridor her naturally brisk pace thwarted by the shuffle of a patient in front attached to a portable drip. There was insufficient room to overtake, and she could see Carolyn looking at her watch in an irritated state.

She returned to the office and desk putting Carolyn's file in the bottom draw and kicking it shut before swivelling around in her chair to look out of the window until the next client arrived.

* * *

Weaving around the bustle of ambulances drop offs and medical staff returning from their lunch hour, Carolyn grabbed her cigarette packet. She had planned to wait until she got to her car, but couldn't, so took her place near to the small, disparate troop of ashen-faced patients and staff puffing away amongst piles of discarded butts.

She took a long, welcome drag and ignored the gaze of a man walking towards her, arms full of soft toys and blue foil balloons steering his heavily pregnant wife towards the entrance.

He turned around again to give Carolyn a second glance as

his wife, clad in a toothpaste-stained velour dressing gown grimacing with discomfort waddled in front and entered the revolving door. Always validated by the male gaze, in that moment Carolyn felt a sudden wave of relief and appreciation for her lithe, taut body and unspoilt, firm skin. She would, she decided with a small surge of enthusiasm go to the gym tomorrow and run hard and fast on the treadmill and then work hard on her abs.

In her hand were the property details of the house in Maltham she and her husband would be viewing later. The impressive scale and proximity to a health club and golf course prompted small approving nods as she absorbed the layout properly for the first time, noting the Juliet balcony off the master bedroom, the free-standing bath and sleek, steel kitchen units.

Already, she was welcoming the mental distraction that would come with an entirely unnecessary refurbishment project, feeling brighter as she answered her husband's call.

"Carolyn where have you been? I've been trying to get hold of you – the house viewing has been put forward to 2pm"

"Well, how could I know that? I'm at the gym – setting off now."

She looked at her watch and eyed the build-up of Friday afternoon traffic waiting to join the motorway and added

"The property looks good by the way in the pictures – though we'll have to rip out the kitchen to get it up to standard."

"Sure, whatever. You've got about half an hour, but we can start without you."

"No, you won't start without me, I'll get there as soon as I can. Oh, it has got a proper office hasn't it, I couldn't see it on the floor plan?"

"Yes, it has," he answered wearily. "Just try and get it as soon as you can sweetheart."

He tossed the phone on the passenger seat, a wry smile and shake of the head over her latest preoccupation with a home office. As someone whose routine was highly unlikely to deviate from the ingrained triumvirate of gym, holidays and restaurants it was entirely unnecessary in his opinion.

Yet as with all of her fads – usually expensive, all-consuming and very temporary, he knew better than to pass comment, the small relief he felt when she sounded more positive and agreeable always outweighed any inclination to upset the apple cart.

9

St Jean -de- Ruel, France, July 2000

David Steadman knew as he followed the patron up two flights of stairs in this lift-free venue that the room would not be to his taste but was still unprepared for the level of disappointment.

In the run up to this trip he had heard much breathless patter about the legendary Le Midi de Nuit hotel in St Jean de Ruel, its quirks, charm and preservation of the oldest customs and family lineage that stretched back to the 18th century, blah bloody blah.

And now he was here hot and exhausted having travelled 800 miles across France to spend a week in what resembled his great aunt's spare bedroom.

The homely, cosy aesthetic was the antithesis of the flashy venues he normally chose with their fully functioning windows and air con. Here, trying to open one of the aged, peeling shutters had already involved a lengthy demonstration from the patron who then stood over him to appraise his attempt at the curious wrist flick. It was a feat of precision and timing that had left sweat pouring down his back and into the crevices, dripping down legs encased in thick denim.

Compounding matters was the fact his room only had a toilet and sink. He would need to use the separate bathroom at the end of the corridor to shower or bathe, an unbelievable oversight in his mind, that left him almost speechless.

Oblivious to his turmoil, another beaming member of staff left a long iron key for this purpose on the small pile of thin towels at the end of his single bed. Once he'd had time to digest the reality, he did what he always did and took action calling reception where attempts to resurrect a few remembered French phrases made way for volume and barked instructions demanding that he must change rooms immediately.

Unused to any sort of dissent from the guests, the patron had found herself in unfamiliar territory but remained polite and good-natured. Eventually it was established there were no spare rooms because the hotel was full due to the Millennium celebrations that weekend. The only alternative was to see if he could share number 17 occupied by Gavin Smee – the one male in his party who had a twin room and spare bed.

He didn't know Gavin Smee and in was in no mood to have a new roommate. In terms of inconvenience and compromise it left him no better off anyway and he sat dejectedly on the bed with the bathroom key in his large, sweaty palm resisting every urge in his being to hurl it out the window.

Yet, in truth, his anger and frustration were rooted more deeply with the real damage done back in England just before he left for the trip. He turned on his mobile phone to confront a flurry of missed calls, texts and voice messages all from his wife, a continuation of that morning's row, which itself had been an overspill from the drink-fuelled slanging match the night before.

Scrolling through them, he realised there would be no reprieve from the onslaught which had become more visceral as the day progressed. One rambling message lasting four minutes as she called him a useless piece of shit 56 times.

The last text message said: "It's your bloody fault we can't adopt a child so sort something out or I swear to god I will DO SOMETHING."

"And it's your fault we can't conceive darling," he punched each letter with such force that the tip of his finger stayed white for some seconds and trembled over the send button in hesitation.

Mindful of the state she was in he deleted it and threw the phone on the bed. He took off his saturated top, grabbed his washbag and retrieved the bathroom key that had landed under the wardrobe.

He opened the bathroom door cautiously, half expecting to interrupt someone using the toilet. To his relief, the simple room with dark wooden floors was better than he expected though he resented having to traipse down the corridor semi naked to access it. Furthermore, the ageing bath couldn't comfortably accommodate his broad, six-foot frame. Feet resting on the taps he immersed most of his body in the warm water and breathed in the first bit of comfort in the last 24 hours. He shut his eyes and prayed for all of this to be over.

"Now as we all know the Maltham Herald chose not to send a reporter or a photographer this year."

The town's current mayor John Brawley was holding court in the hotel's restaurant, standing up as he always did on account of his five-foot five frame to address the members of his local town's twinning committee.

Gavin Smee shook his head animatedly to make his disapproval known.

"Yes, I know," the mayor said, observing him. "We're all very disappointed by the decision particularly as this is Millennial year and our hosts have put together such a varied itinerary. However, all is not lost..."

He smiled milking a dramatic pause as his eyes morphed into little sparkly slits in the fleshy expanse of his face.

"We are extremely fortunate to have David Steadman with us who has stepped into the breech at very short notice as our official photographer. Now for those of us who may not already know, David and his wife..."

He looked over for a prompt.

"Carolyn," Gavin Smee obliged to David's surprise.

"Sorry, David and *Carolyn* will be moving to The Glades at the end of the month from London and are expected to play a very active role in our community both with their business and charitable interests which I know from talking to David earlier are extremely varied."

Impressed murmurs milled around the table. A collective realisation that this still relatively young man had the means to reside in Maltham's most exclusive address had chimed with a group always alert to new well-heeled and connected contacts.

"Now, David's day job is in advertising but in a former life he did in fact channel his inner David Bailey as a staff photographer at what I believe is now a defunct magazine called Melody Maker?" he said it with a questioning tone, not expecting the others to have heard of it either which their blank faces confirmed.

"And I'm told by a reliable source that it was very cool and trendy."

The last two words were delivered with a stilted wiggle of his hips and quote mark gestures and David Steadman found himself wanting to laugh in spite of his mounting turmoil.

"I thought I'd mention all this just in case any of you were in any doubt about his creative credentials."

Gavin Smee's fake laugh filled an expectant pause.

"So, if you can all raise your glasses, I'd like to make the first toast to David and welcome him officially to St Jean de Ruel and to Maltham's twinning committee and to promise him that if it's anything like the previous years this week will be a good one."

The tall, tanned man doused in Dior Fahrenheit acknowledged this with a glass of peach liqueur and his usual winning smile. Being the centre of attention in a buzzing social hub was familiar territory for David Steadman but he was struggling tonight, low on both energy and the inclination to return the interest shown from his companions, only too aware that most of it came with an agenda.

As he'd anticipated, the next four courses were spent diplomatically batting away unwelcome business offers and answering several variations of the same questions. These mostly sought more detail on how he'd made his money as well as free advice from the various self-anointed entrepreneurs round the table who didn't have the budgets to engage his services properly. While drink was helping to take the edge of his low-grade boredom and the deeper anxiety of his domestic woes it still wasn't enough and as the evening progressed, he became ever more certain that he needed a deeper release.

He took the distraction of the cheese trolley and the laboured and protracted decisions that ensued as his cue to leave, telling the others that after a long day of driving he needed some fresh air and early night.

Walking past the heaving tables in this long dining room and swell of easy laughter he stepped out into the still warm night to the sound of crickets and the river's permanently rousing soundtrack with some relief.

He didn't usually like to be alone, but right now it felt like the greatest luxury, a reprieve from all the effort and forced sociability, of the evening, everything calm and simple. He started walking with no particular plan or destination in mind, hearing distant laughter and snippets of conversation from unseen friends and couples conveying a kind of carefree joy de vivre that he very much lacked which made him feel sad and envious which wasn't his usual state.

It was still only 10 pm and with no intention of returning to his tiny room any earlier than he had to he headed on autopilot to a bar at the other end of the village called the Blue Parrott.

On entering he was hit by thick Smoke and Grace Jones played at full volume. It was a slick operation run by a young team deftly milking the passing tourist trade while looking after the regulars. He particularly liked the elegant, minimalist décor and the uniformity of the rows of bottles and stacked glasses displayed behind the bar which resonated with his own obsessive tidiness.

He ordered a brandy and positioned himself on one of the stools at the bar within eye balling distance of two young English woman, probably in their early 20s. Neither were as striking as his wife, few people were, but in the moment, he found the contrast particularly appealing – minimal make up, loose unstyled hair and casual clothes a certain effortlessness that could never be said about Carolyn's more glamourous, stylised appearance. The irony of marrying his ideal woman when his head was still routinely turned by those offering such a physical contrast wasn't lost on him.

He considered checking her latest messages but decided not to spoil an evening that was finally showing signs of improvement. His interest had been further piqued by the pair's confident, well-spoken voices which in his vast and varied sexual experience had so often equated to some of his most debauched encounters.

When he finally joined them, they were more interesting company than he'd expected though expectations hadn't been high and talk of travel, ambitions and coveted internships was nothing more than background noise anyway: by now his eyes and mind were fixed only on the physical and specifically the logistics of how and where.

He took another swig of drink as thoughts of his single bed in his shoebox hotel room jostled with a fantasy of no holds bar fornication. Even in his desperate state he knew it would be a bad idea to take either or both back to the hotel with the likelihood of being seen by someone in his party, an indiscretion that would jar with the carefully constructed respectability.

"So, what do you do then," said Girl One briefly interrupting his dilemma.

"A pilot." He always lied when pursuing women and favoured especially random answers because he enjoyed the challenge of making whatever fiction he'd concocted sound plausible, and it eased the boredom until the main event.

Such activity had become less frequent in recent years, but he was reminded of how much he enjoyed this well-worn game and its banter and expectation which with his better than average looks and self-confidence came with a high success rate. He also knew that these two were very much his sweet spot. In their impressionable, less jaded eyes, he was old enough to convey a certain sophistication but still young enough to be devoid of the seedier undertones that he'd carry in ten years 'time.

He was testing the waters now with the one that for convenience was closest to him and appealed more simply for that reason, a stroke of the arm, tap of the thigh, leaning closer, compliments shifting to the more outrageous remarks he always seemed to get away with as the distant bleep of a text message reminded him to turn off his phone.

"Wife trying to get hold of you?" she asked more amused than judgemental flicking back tousled layers of tawny, expensively highlighted hair.

His paused but as she stroked his wedding ring with the mutual exchange of a knowing look his marital status didn't seem to an issue.

Round the back of the Blue Parrot in a small gravelly car park home to rubbish bins and a sleeping cat his hands found their way down the back of her combat trousers. The feel of taut unfamiliar flesh fed a surge of arousal as the last layers of control and inhibition surrendered and he sated the craving that had been festering all night. He drunk in the intensity of the moment and its unconscious oblivion that could nullify any worries and responsibility however briefly.

And then nothing. As always that instant switch from euphoria to emptiness as fast as the build-up been protracted and a desperation to get away from a person that now left him cold and whose name he'd forgotten. He made his excuses and left.

* * *

Sorry about today (and last night) it was the drink, but you know why ....

I love you sooooooooooo much Caz XXX

Sitting on his hotel bed he reread the message several times feeling an odd mix of guilt and relief that at least his wife had finally calmed down. Tears were welling and he knew in that moment that he would never feel the same way about anyone else and that he would have to do something, anything to make her happy to give her what she wanted and make this stop once and for all.

10

St Jean de Ruel, France, July 2000

9.30 am

That morning Jacque Renaud drank his usual hot chocolate, which today came with a pale blue macaron. He was dressed in his best outfit - a second birthday present from his grandmother – which reflected her traditional tastes: Long corduroy shorts, a matching top embroidered with toy soldiers and a pair of red-t bar shoes. It was a get up that came out for most family or village celebrations with today's religious festival being no exception. At 9 am he was sent on his way with his older cousins and strict instructions to hold their hands at all times and not get his outfit dirty.

11.30 am

And then he saw him. A small figure under three-foot-tall dressed in his Sunday best wandering from the main street's festival celebrations down a side road which fed into a mesh of back streets and would end at the sprawling Bois de Foret.

David Steadman wasn't religious, but he did believe in fate. Had he not agreed to be the town council's photographer he would never have been at a festival with the masses celebrating a gilt Jesus but here he was, and it was all for a reason.

Lying in his bed the previous night, the man wondered what he was really doing on this trip; after the long boring meal and empty sex with stranger he felt especially low and flat as his usual basic pleasures fell short. He knew why.

Carolyn's hysteria was unsettling him; the flare up in her eating disorder, the desperation for children. For the first time he found himself looking at her bare, morning face, free of the usual cosmetics and thinking she didn't look well. Her sporadic threats to harm herself had had segued from an empty, theatrical white noise to a more ominous sounding warning that grated on him whether he was work or in the gym or with someone he shouldn't be. What if she really did do something drastic?

When his house key went in the lock tension loomed inside of him as to what he might discover; this wasn't the self-made life he had hustled hard for, and it demanded a seismic intervention to repair it.

He glanced around him checking the notable absence of a concerned parent and the droves of preoccupied locals and tourists, high on revelry.

His own group, inflated by the arrival of their French hosts was equally distracted. With the figurine of Jesus yet to make an appearance, Maltham's town clerk Gavin Smee was the centre of attention suffering a hypoglycaemic attack, slumped against a lamppost, head lolling and legs outstretched. His plight had drawn a crowd that bellowed loud, incomprehensible instructions and jostled to rouse him with little shakes to the shoulder while trying to feed him something sticky and sweet from the nearby cafe.

The man sensed an opportunity. Hand in his pockets he turned his back on the mayhem, sloping off unnoticed to follow the child who had already made good progress down the Rue de Stade. With all the action and crowds converged onto the village centre this back street was deserted. Usually buzzing little outlets were now dark and shuttered for the festivities, with all sounds muted as if a switch had been turned off, bar the soft tread of two pairs of feet and distant buzz of traffic. He looked behind him saw nothing and picked up his pace.

It was an odd kind of pursuit really, with no need to hide from the oblivious target as the pair passed stray dogs and the kind of shabbier anomalous outlets that usually fringed the outskirts of these small, rural towns. A beige emporium selling orthopaedic aids flashed by as did a photographic studio with its window full of dated portraits and dead flies that had collected around frames in need of a good clean.

On the other side of the street stood an elegant and old fashioned papeterie with some 20 empty wine bottles stacked by some bins outside. It was a surprisingly tatty scene which the man observed with little interest distracted more by his reflection in the shop windows which he would catch intermittently and kept being disappointed by.

He was good looking and aware of it, though not especially vain but this tired face with the emergence of frown lines and dark circles didn't chime with the image in his head and concerned him. Looking a certain way, the way he was used to looking, seemed to make life easy and he didn't want that to change. He could only attribute this slight decline to the strain of the past year, the house move and cycle of failed IVF attempts. All was compounded by a mild hangover and poor night's sleep in his single bed in his tiny, hot room with shutters that wouldn't open where he had sweated and wrestled with his conscience into the early hours.

Carolyn was always reminding him of the importance of a good skincare routine which bored him immensely, but perhaps she had a point, and then he considered how odd it was to be thinking about moisturiser while in pursuit of a stranger's child in a strange town.

As he slowed his pace to accommodate his target's tiny stride he wondered if his mind was straying because the idea was so half hearted it was about to be abandoned anyway. Or was it simply because he was feeling too comfortable and in control that the enormity of what he could be about to do didn't even need to fully consume him.

He settled on the latter. Recent events reminded him that by and large, he felt invincible and in control, blasé enough to have given no thought to how his absence would be explained to the rest of his group, which given his elevated status within it would have already been noticed he assumed.

Drawn to his energy, success and relative youth, the grey, parochial collective with their paunch and receding hairlines would swallow anything he told them, just as the girl, from last night had done and everyone else did.

As the shops petered out, a small cemetery appeared on the left. It was typical of the sort that fringe small rural communities - sprawling plots belonging to generations of the same family enshrined in large, elaborate marble tombs. Some dated back to the 1890s he noticed and if he hadn't been otherwise engaged, he would have looked around it because he always found cemeteries to be great levellers, especially abroad. Carolyn hated them and always stayed in the car, but for him, they were useful reminders that for all of life's preoccupations, we all end up as dust.

An empty playground came up on the left still failing to divert the boy's focus from his determined mission. Only a cat lolling on a sunny step briefly stirred by the approaching footsteps prompted a second glance before the youngster resumed his steady plod.

As they approached the first road, the man picked up his pace, protectively but there was no traffic, and the boy reached the other side unharmed as the environment transitioned into something more rural with a stonier, stubbier ground.

Here the toddler's progress finally stalled. Small feet and a rudimentary sense of balance starting to struggle with the uneven, unpredictable surface as slips and falls became more frequent. The river and the imposing bois de foret backdropped by fir-tree mountains loomed. In this more desolate scene, it was easier to skew the narrative; now the man was simply protector whose intervention would be critical anyway to prevent the inevitable harm the boy would come to left to his own devices or so he told himself.

His rhythm fractured, the child was now still and aimless for the first time looking around as if unsure what to do next as David Steadman caught him up, smiling broadly to put him at ease.

"Hello, little man."

The boy looked up at him warily but not especially scared or phased by the stranger, more inquisitive. As the adult knelt to look at him properly, he took in the mop of dark brown curly hair, large intense eyes, pink face moist with sweat and curiously old-fashioned ensemble. His long socks had bunched under grazed knees with the scuffed, dusty edges of his T-bar red shoes further testament to his excursion.

This contrasted with the gleaming polish of the main part of the shoe which must have been recently applied. He could see that he was well cared for and for the first time the boy's family and a life that existed beyond this encounter crossed his mind. Guilt and unease could be swiftly countered though, and he was electrified by the possibilities of his find. A child so young, not yet forming proper words, random sounds hinting at the character to come, a blank canvas, formed but unformed, able to be moulded into whatever he wanted, whatever *she* wanted: Too young to remember.

The boy proffered a grazed palm for inspection and David picked him up with no resistance. Tired from his exertions he was ready to be carried, however unfamiliar the arms. He was deceptively heavy, but the man didn't mind as he traipsed along the edge of the river enjoying the feeling of the child's small hand resting on his upper arm and the sun which shone hard and bright in a cloudless sky. Both pairs of eyes fell on the butterflies dancing around the rushes, flashes of yellow, purples and cornflower blue, bold and vivid against the muted green and brown palette of the surroundings. The clear water exposed the brown and pinks of its rocky bed while an incessant chain of ripples and agitations across the surface spoke of the varied life inside, sudden, rapid movements that kept the toddler's attention.

It occurred to him how normal the abnormal can look. How this scene would appear innocuous to a passing stranger when it was anything but, not that there was anyone in the vicinity. It was as if life had temporarily shifted elsewhere to one central street as he sat on the bench with his thoughts, the implications and excuses now competing for supremacy. He was very aware he was on a precipice and that all of this could still be explained away easily with no suspicion or judgment.

He had simply found him here and was heading back to the police station. A safety net, an undercurrent of normality, plausibility, and justification that could stop the episode unravelling into the drama with its risk and ramifications was still there. Just. But he knew in his heart that it was too late and that he would not return to Carolyn without him. He kept the boy on his lap, one arm firmly around his waist, while the other retrieved his phone from the trouser pocket and opened his latest messages, all from Carolyn.

Head banging from last night, but I've got ready and will drag myself to gym x

Bloke on reception flirting with me.... again - the one with the nose!! .... might complain!

He smiled appreciating this burst of normality amid the rising self-created drama though it soon faded as he read the final message sent 20 minutes ago.

Jesus Christ, David why can't I be happy?

He stared blankly ahead, his strong, secure hold containing the ceaseless wriggles of his new charge before looking over at the slate models of wolves standing at the edge of the forest. He had noticed similar versions planted on the edge of the river from his hotel window and was told over dinner the reason for their presence. Head back and eyes shut he took a deep breath enjoying the warmth of the sun on his face, listening to the repetitive but relaxing birdsong, playing on a loop. Like squeezing the last drops of sleep once the alarm has sounded this was a final simple hit of comfort.

He took off one of the boy's red shoes which filled his palm and ran his thumb along the stitching of the T-bar strap and felt the moist leather inside. Carrying the toddler, he walked over to the forest opening and into the clean, dark coolness and placed the shoe on the ground, rearranging it several times, on bracken partially covering with leaves.

Whatever the variant, the position always seemed to be contrived and at odds with the sense of wrenched abandonment he was trying to convey. Eventually he went back to the bench and threw it hard preferring how it landed and left it there.

Jacque Renaud looked down at his exposed white sock with a puzzled expression and back at the stranger carrying him.

. . .

"Guy – it's David, are you alone?"

"Oh god, what is it now?" his brother asked wearily.

"I need a favour; a big one – but you owe me you know that. You need to listen to the following instructions: I don't have time for questions you just need to answer me."

"Ben's passport – how old is in the picture?"

Pause.

"I dunno, six or eight months?"

"Ok, that's fine. You need to post it to this address in France"

"David what the bloody hell is going on?"

"No time to explain; have you got a pen? Write this down: Hotel Campanile, 2 Olivier de la Danse, 21160 Marsannay-la-Côte, France. You've gotta send it immediately no messing about."

11

Maltham, England, May 2002

From the bay window of her living room on a grey Monday morning, Valerie Hobson observes a familiar scene. As always at about 8 am, a man in his mid -30s hurries out of the property opposite, an armful of matching leather bags and folders quickly despatched onto the passenger seat of his sportscar.

She isn't sure what he does but even without the telling backdrop of his large, detached property in the most monied part of town he has the swagger of the successful who is impatient for more.

He's soon followed by a woman, perhaps a little younger, holding the hand of a young boy, three or four years old. The child, short and sturdy is drowning in the fuss of the local prep school's elaborate maroon and gold school uniform and is marshalled into the back seat of her Range Rover, his thick dark hair that wants to curl has been gelled heavily into a side parting.

The mother, who Valerie concedes, is attractive, if in a rather obvious, modern way, is wearing white jeans that expose a wisp of pink lace underwear whenever she bends, while a baggy top hangs off a taut, tanned shoulder. A large side slit that ends just under the bra further reveals a toned flat stomach seemingly unfettered by childbirth. All in all, she surmises out loud to herself in this empty house, the look may seem casual but is highly impractical for any meaningful task and designed simply to show off a lean body and attract attention.

She takes in the five-inch-high wedged sandals and the limited interaction between the mother and child. The boy looks non plussed by the prospect of another day at his very expensive school as the woman tries out a few variations of an impromptu hair bun in the reflection of the car window, twirling thick, glossy strands absently around her fingers before abandoning the efforts and leaving it down.

Ms Hobson does not have children herself or a husband, but it is not a scene that stirs any untapped unfulfillment or envy.

Financially, she has her own comfortable existence, from both family money and a long, steady career in the civil service which has given her a substantial property filled with understated quality furniture and the freedom to live without any real pressures. Yet cracks have emerged.

A relative success and seniority in her professional life brought purpose, respect and deference and usually the last word. Post retirement, she finds the world far less malleable and cooperative. It's one in which her forthright and lively opinions coupled with a propensity for condescending lectures tend to grate on others and are now only indulged by very oldest and closest friends.

Under the sharper judgement and more anonymous dealings and interactions with the wider public, she has become an increasingly less tolerated irrelevance, the sort of person, who on occasion, in the GP surgery or a garden centre causes others to roll their eyes as she launches into some protracted explanation to the bored, blank face of the person at the counter or behind her in the queue.

The woman is too sharp to be oblivious to the shift in status and diminishing respect and wonders if all of this has fuelled her preoccupation with this new family at The Glades though tries not to analyse it too much. Younger and busier with their bigger, bolder stamp of new money, they are sufficiently alien from herself and her own existence to pique her interest like some guilty pleasure on the television that she pretends not to watch.

And now her eyes are drawn to the back seat of the wife's car. The boy, staring out the window, she reckons must be a weekly border as she only sees him leave Monday and return Friday. In between, though, there is a steady flow of visitors – a mobile beautician usually Wednesdays and Fridays, gardener on Monday, while similarly aged loud and glamourous friends come and go.

The regular weekend parties that migrate to the garden of a warmer evening provide the best opportunity for judgement from their one-woman audience. Distant drink-fuelled shrieks of jarred heavily with the solitude of her front room but the arrivals and departures keep her shrewd mind transfixed. She likes to think she can get the measure of the friendship group dynamics even from the most fleeting observations: the tall woman with the long, red hair who always puts a clingy, territorial arm around her other half as they approach the front door is particularly intriguing – her beaming face drops instantly as they leave the property, struggling with the competition of her peer group.

Hours can pass watching all of this, save for the odd tea or toilet break, with only the ending of a television programme reminding her how long she had been stood there. And now Val

Hobson's eyes follow the woman's Range Rover as it reverses out of the drive stirring gravel and dust. Loud dance music sounds out, volume rising as the window rolls down which makes her sigh and shake her head at the stridence of it all compounded by the personalised number plate.

"Common as muck" she says solemnly to herself.

In fact, the couple's inferior class was already established the previous week after she opened her window to try and catch a loud argument between in the driveway. It confirmed the estuary twang, she suspected and the fact they were not her sort of person, though few are nowadays other than her immediate circle which is why it continues to shrink so rapidly.

She turns back to her own life and takes in the room which is tidied and ordered to such an extent that even she feels stifled and reluctant to touch or disturb anything.

As she sits in her olive-green armchair, smartened with a tapestry throw, she rallies hard not to let the flatness she feels consume her now that this part of her morning routine has ended.

Thoughts of another long day that must be filled somehow always feel overwhelming at this point when she allows herself to dwell on it and the TV remains off.

8.15. Good god. She stretches her legs and arms one by one and fidgets in the chair. She wishes she could sleep in longer, but a certain discipline and routine instilled from her working life compounded by an inability to relax prevents it. Often, she awakes at 4am eking out a couple more restless hours until she rises at 7.

8.22. Still too early for her morning coffee so she picks up the new copy of the Radio Times and fetches her fluorescent marker pen from the tin on the sideboard to highlight her viewing itinerary. As someone who knows the schedules pretty much by rote, the process isn't necessary but seeing her choices under a wash of pink gives her something to look forward toto while reading the programme blurbs, cast lists and reviews which she inevitably ends up doing at can help pass more time.

She tuts at having forgotten her ruler which she fetches from the same tin. By the time she has finished the page is more blushed than black and white but with the growing number of new channels showing repeats of her favourite sit coms it's inevitable and not something she's going to bother feeling guilty about.

* * *

When she wakes in her armchair, she notices her pen has dropped on the floor, lidless with a drying nib. To her relief, the time has crept to 11.50 am but it is still too early for lunch and to switch the television on. She tries to keep it off until about 1pm, one of those self-enforced and pointless rules, that she has no idea why she bothers to adhere.

12

England, August 2017

A slew of fundraising dinners punctuated Maltham's social calendar attracting the usual core crowd who expected their philanthropy and community-mindedness to be recorded in the local paper. It was a largely reciprocal arrangement, substantial picture spreads of the same faces quaffing and cheque-holding had remained a reliably easy page filler and was known to have a positive effect on sales with those photographed often buying several copies.

Sending staff to cover such events, however, remained the bane of a newsroom, particularly the Partridge Dinner, a late summer fundraiser held at the town's historic Castle with its 12 am finish and requirement for black tie or ballgown. The paper's old timers who rarely left their house after 8pm were non-starters while the revolving door of junior staff tended to struggle with the more arcane protocols and had better things to do on a Friday night.

In a diary inked only with her facials and therapy sessions

Leah did not. Yet as someone who at least appeared as if she might have a life, the journalist saw the value in pretending to shuffle or cancel imaginary appointments in an apparent show of dedication and willingness that didn't go unnoticed by the management and scored easy points.

For once, she had unexpected competition. Keen for some respite from the confines of the bed and breakfast where he currently lived, Dave Garland had also volunteered to attend for a free night out. It was an awkward offer discussed behind the editor's closed doors with the consensus reached that the chief sub editor's poor hygiene and general weirdness made him an unsuitable public 'face' of the paper.

"He wouldn't bother making notes during the speeches; he'd be out having a fag," chipped in the editor's PA, Sue Lansford whose opinion carried surprising weight when it came to resolving these more offbeat personnel matters. "And I can't think for one minute he has his own tuxedo."

"No, I can't either," agreed the editor. "Right, well that's that then; I'll tell Leah to get her glad rags on."

"And perhaps to crack a smile while she's at it."

"Oh, come on Sue!"

"I'm sorry Peter I know you're very fond of her, but does she always have to be bloody sullen? Stomping around the place with a face like thunder thinking she's above everyone else."

The woman crossed her legs exposing a blotchy, swollen ankle as she wriggled in her seat.

"Of course, she never had any time for me the first time round and even less so now and she has been very rude to the women on reception, very, rude – demanding they fetch her Mars Bars when she's on a deadline as if she's editing Fleet Street's finest.

"She has her issues Sue," said the editor wearily, used to defending his favourite enfant terrible. "What really matters is that she's actually a bloody good reporter. Her abilities don't go unnoticed, you know, several people have praised the quality of writing since she returned."

"And she was very unpleasant with Nicola Prescot the other day," continued the PA rarely interested in the finer points of editorial quality with months of festering indignation towards the journalist finally getting an airing.

"Nicola Prescott? Now where do I know that name from?" said Peter.

"Oh, you know - only the reporter that worked here for two years in the late 90s; Obviously didn't make such an impression as the lovely Leah. She's now the police press officer and told me that the other day Leah was very aggressive when they met up for the crime briefing."

Peter removed his glasses and rubbed his tired, red eyes.

"Ok Sue, you've had your rant and your feedback is noted; I'll have a word, but for now, if you'd like you to resume your duties..."

The woman huffily snatched her coffee cup and papers and made a protracted job of returning her chair to the back of the room. He sighed deeply as he eyed her retreat with her arse-chewing slacks that had lost as much elasticity as the body inside.

Sue's devotion to him and the newspaper had seen her continue working for pittance well beyond the age of retirement with no real perks or pay rise. The trade-off, however, was that in common with most of the paper's difficult staff, she required careful handling and the odd indulgence of her outbursts which could still test even his patience.

When the older woman returned to the newsroom, Leah noticed her flushed face and left eye twitching for England, the usual hallmark of some lost altercation, all of which appealed to her warped and childish sense of humour. She smirked at the screen as the perfect pun materialised to finish her headline as the other woman bristled at her desk.

As the usual jobsworth surveyed her press card with the same level of scrutiny he applied every week, Leah took in the town council chamber's high ceiling and dark wood panelled walls, plush maroon carpets and velvet curtains.

It was a luxe gentlemen club aesthetic that she appreciated more now than the first time around as a 20 something, though it was a level of style and grandiose disproportionate to the reed thin debates that took place within its walls, heavy with repetition and pettiness.

As she climbed the stairs to the upper gallery, she wondered how many times she had heard the same long running sagas and spurious reasons proffered to deny affordable houses from the mortgage-free members of the planning committee who resented anything too cheap or modern to blight the view from their two-acre piles.

A few residents had taken their seats, breaking off from low voiced conversation to eye her and her notepad as she took her usual position in the centre of an empty front row, the whole of which had been optimistically reserved for the press. Staff and councillors began to trickle in, and she returned Vince Dunkett's smile and Gavin Smee's efficient nod, noticing how harassed Ros looked clutching an overstuffed folder to her matronly bust. The press officer settled in her new seat next to the chairman, ready to take the minutes, the latest duty to be offloaded onto to her ever-expanding remit.

A few slightly younger members Leah didn't recognise followed as did some familiar faces from before, now stooped, crustier versions of their 2002 selves rearranging their papers with the kind of bustling intensity of the self-important.

In a world of anonymity, where seemingly little control existed it had always struck her how this sorry tribe were rare masters of their destiny helming their little pocket of influence. Perhaps that was the answer to contentment – aiming low and staying local, though of course, the real challenge was being satisfied with that.

She pressed record on her Dictaphone, so she would be covered when her mind wandered from proceedings as it often did. Gavin Smee stood and cleared his throat.

"Before we get to the main agenda this evening, I would like to remind everyone that in honour of the 20th anniversary of Maltham town council's twinning arrangement with St Jean de Ruel we have a temporary display in the council hall which I'd encourage as many people as possible to view."

He paused and looked up at Leah as he often did when making announcement at these meetings to see if she was making notes all in the mistaken belief that he had any influence over what ended up in her report.

He continued: "There's a selection of original photographs and we have the old editions on loan from the Maltham Herald which of course feature every report from every visit starting from the inaugural one in 1997 to this year so do make sure you take the time to have a look."

Indecipherable murmurs came from the handful of people near her.

"Thank you, Chairman," he added looking towards his colleague and making a small bowing gesture before sitting down and ticking something off on a list in his notebook with a small self-satisfied smile.

The meeting passed with predictable form. At the request of the chairman, someone had brought more details on how a proposed social housing development could affect the habitat of the sand lizard population thought to be on the site. The findings reaffirmed suspicions that the impact would be very detrimental indeed on this species and as such, the committee would be making a formal objection to the development.

Afterwards out of curiosity Leah made a detour to the twinning archive display. The 1997 edition of the Maltham Herald with its gushing introductory feature on Jean de Ruel's history had set the tone for the breathless commentary that had followed since.

The photo spread of that first visit revealed a maiden contingency considerably smaller from the size it had swollen to in more recent years. Among the usual platitudes the St Jean de Ruel Mayor of that year had expressed his condolences over the death of the Princess Diana, just a week previously. Leah absorbed it all with a mild professional interest comparing writing styles of various reporters and noting the inclusion of some politically incorrect clangers that would be off limits now even in the Herald.

It was the July 2000 coverage of the visit that made her jaw drop with its series of photos credited to David Steadman revealing a link she had been oblivious to.

She scoured the report and noticed a small photo in the corner of page seven showing the man himself, tanned and smiling sandwiched between the then mayor and a slightly younger-looking Gavin Smee in the familiar setting of the Hotel Le Midi de Nuit's restaurant as thoughts of Jacque Renard flooded her mind.

"So, the millennial edition has caught your eye," said Gavin Smee loitering nearby.

"I didn't know David Steadman was on the twinning visit in 2000," she said trying to sound casual.

"Oh yes the one and only time though; he came as our

photographer because ....and you're not going to like this I'm afraid – the Herald didn't send anyone to cover the trip – I think the excuse was that you had too much on covering the millennium events locally, though it was a very disappointing, *very* disappointing."

"Before my time Gavin." she responded quickly not wanting to be drawn on the 20-year-old editorial decision that still riled him. "Anyway, I didn't know he was ever on the twinning committee."

"He wasn't. If I remember correctly was at the time he and his wife were just about to move to Maltham from Ealing, I think, but don't quote me on that. He was considering getting involved with the council and various local groups, but his business commitments made it difficult for him to find the time and then of course events took over... you know, with Tom and everything."

A long pause lingered as she processed the implications.

"Why do you ask"? said Gavin finally.

"Oh, no reason."

"Actually, what I do remember," continued the town clerk. "Was that he had to leave early about two days before the end, some sort of family emergency, I think. God, drama just follows some people around, doesn't it?"

"Oh, yeah?" Leah looked at him willing more revelations and detail.

"I can't remember the specifics; just that one minute he was there and the next he wasn't."

13

Maltham, England August 2017

Leah's day-to-day style was casual, but an interest in scouring second-hand designer outlets meant she had an extensive wardrobe of labels such as Alexander McQueen and Hugo Boss to draw from when the occasion demanded it.

For that evening's Partridge dinner, it was to be the former's black trousers with braces over a Chloe pink lacey top off the shoulder with voluminous puff sleeves. It had always reminded her of the top half of Princess Diana's wedding dress and the resulting look was a fusion of feminine and androgyny, she carried off well with her model height and broad shoulders. Furthermore, a facial had plumped an already good complexion so that despite her still troubled sleep, she looked good as she walked the long approach to the castle that was lit up in honour of the night's event.

She liked the fading light and fresher air of late summer evening. The breeze stirred the medicinal scents of lemon balm and basil sensory gardens which lapped the main building as a rising throb of chatter propelled her to the main entrance where Nicola Prescott with bad VPL stood with her kilt-wearing husband. As someone who always bore a grudge, Leah strutted past the pair feeling infinitely superior and thinking how ridiculous they looked.

Inside, the hundred or so guests, a mass of black tie and crushed velvet twittered away in their respective bubbles of animated conversation. The most feverish displays, she noticed, were reserved for those orbiting the local MP, who along with the mayor, was always the star attraction at these gatherings. For Leah, joining one of these clusters was inconceivable. Others seemed to do it with ease, taking the cue of collective laughter to integrate themselves seamlessly, but she simply fiddled with her phone, waiting for someone to approach which was why it was a relief to see Ros heading her way as a suitably undemanding social buffer.

"Doesn't it all look delightful – so pretty – did you see the tealights, lovely?" said the press officer gesturing outside.

Leah nodded taking in what stood before her.

In a rare concession to glamour, Ros had applied some make up but in common with those who rarely wear it, the effect was very stark; a strong red lipstick and pale eyeshadow which rather than enhancing her features simply highlighted their shortfalls. A heavy matte foundation, a shade too dark skimmed the edge of her jawline while the ends of her limp, mousey bob had acquired a feeble curl. As usual she wore a low-cut strapless dress that exposed too much pale flab which had a terrible pitted texture. It was an anomaly that always puzzled Leah, as to why someone who spent every day of their life swaddled in draping smocks and cardigans dressed so revealingly at these staid black-tie functions.

Seemingly oblivious to her own sartorial faux pas, Ros looked Leah up and down, eyes pausing over the trousers and flicker of midriff without comment but obvious judgement. The two women made small talk that centred mostly on Ros's rare criticism of her employers at the prospect of facing another weekend catching up on her workload.

"You ought to say something."

Leah, knew, however she was wasting her breath; advice was pointless. The woman was an exasperating hybrid of naivety, ignorance and pomposity - usually wrong but could never be told otherwise.

"What you have to remember, Leah, is that I am the council's *senior* press officer, even though I'm not actually trained in media relations, so, I'm hardly in a position to be laying down the law now, am I?"

"I didn't know there was a junior one," came Leah's waspish response, well aware it was a department of one.

"What"?

"A junior press officer."

"Well, there isn't, but we thought the title better reflects my experience," said Ros, who of course, was entirely on board with this latest token gesture designed to keep her compliant, while working harder for the same salary

A group milling around a large mahogany table at the back of the room was the distraction she needed, and Leah led the pair towards it to find a display of Carolyn Steadman's book, *A Mother's Story* laid out in a circle like a wreath. A few castle-themed trinkets and paper weights were sprinkled around it along with a note that announced that proceeds of all sales would be going to the Steadman's new charitable foundation. There were no further details as people discussed its contents conspiratorially much of which, Leah noted, focused on the superficial with comments about Carolyn's hair and outfits and home furnishings.

For something to do the journalist flicked through pages she had already seen at the Steadman's house as Ros remained impassive over her shoulder.

"I don't know about you, but I feel just a little bit uneasy with this," said the press officer finally, a fat finger gesturing to the material.

For once Leah agreed but let her continue without comment.

"It's been 15 years, and it all feels a bit like there's no end."

"I suppose that's the point though; there is no real end is there?" said Leah thinking how photogenic Carolyn was, the type of woman who looked good regardless of angle, lighting or level of preparation.

"Well, he's obviously dead, isn't he? Though we should be careful what we say," she said glancing around furtively, I'm pretty sure that David Steadman's here tonight."

"Is he?" Leah looked up from a picture of Carolyn and Tom swathed in cashmere and ice skating in New York.

"What? All this time, no trace whatsoever, what else can we think; oh, it really is a truly horrible business," said Ros.

"No, I mean is David Steadman here tonight?"

"I think I saw him in the other room."

"Is Carolyn with him?" she asked not really sure why. She replaced the book on the top of the pile, leaving a smudge of makeup from her fingers on its cream cover and wondered if it was ever possible to attend any event that was not in some way touched by the saga of Tom Steadman.

"We'd better put this one somewhere else, hadn't we?" said Ros, as if speaking to naughty child, taking the marked book and putting it at the bottom of an alternative pile that had since formed.

Leah watched distractedly. The discovery that David Steadman had been on the trip at the time that Jacque Renard had gone missing was an uneasy development that for the past few days she had been unwilling to address in any meaningful way – upping her time in the gym, running faster, lifting heavier weights and having a litany of beauty treatments, anything to distract from something that for the time being she had no real idea how to confront as if in some ways it was all too much effort in her still fragile state.

Yet delaying any action had also brought an unexpected benefit. Whenever she thought about her new finding in France, she felt a rush of adrenaline akin to the anticipation of a big event or an intense crush. Sitting on this discovery, however implausible it would seem to some, had become a welcome diversion from her usual issues and self-absorption, awakening the numbness and giving her a curious sense of power ready to be unleashed whenever she decided to press the switch.

"Good evening, ladies," David Steadman appeared from nowhere kissing both her and Ros on the cheek. As with most men of a certain age, he looked better for wearing an expensive suit and smelt good as she breathed in the familiar scent of Dior Fahrenheit which she used to wear herself when she was out on the town.

He stared at her as he took a long sip of his champagne which surprised and unnerved her.

"I thought I'd go for something a little different from the usual evening dress," she found herself explaining to fill the pause that wouldn't usually trouble her.

"I like it, it suits you," he smiled, knowing eyes looking her up and down.

"Ladies and gentlemen, if you would like to make your way to the Great Hall," boomed the town crier. "Dinner is served."

The three of them joined the exodus heading to the next room but were swiftly dispersed by the seating plan. It was disappointing for Leah, as David Steadman in a flirtier and more uninhibited state would be ripe for subtle probing. She watched him take his seat at the top table along with the mayor and others who would be giving speeches while she consigned herself to the polite but tedious company of two local solicitors - specialities divorce law and probate - and the Herald's competition winners whose prize was that evening's attendance and her own company.

As always with the Partridge Dinner, the tables were dressed with elaborate bouquets and spanned the width of the room hung with stuffed deer heads and historic portraits. A troupe of young waiting staff of varying speed and enthusiasm appeared from several arched doorways to despatch plates of salmon mousse, a course swiftly followed by the partridge.

True to form, the actual eating of it was delayed until the town crier had relayed the usual story about the dinner's historic origins an embellished yarn that centred on a notable 16th century bishop rescuing a dying partridge on a roadside.

Some five minutes later and as a few murmurs of discontent attested, it was a formality that had become superfluous. Most of these regular attendees were well-versed in the saga and reluctant to hear it again as their food started to go cold.

Weaving through the throng of bodies bobbing awkwardly to the entertainment, Leah headed outside to the castle's courtyard which dripped in the aftermath of a shower.

She shivered slightly as she looked back through the window at the various gauche exploits and libidinous rituals playing out. She was aware that in many ways she had become an observer of life rather than a participant at the heart of the action though it wasn't something that concerned her as other people's idea of fun rarely tallied with her own. She turned back out to the courtyard and sighed deeply looking up the black sky and thinking how everything was simplified at night with detail form and nuance largely smothered in darkness.

"Didn't have you down as a smoker." David Steadman appeared behind her, jacket off, a few shirt buttons undone removing a cigarette from a packet of Dunhill.

"I'm not, just fancied some air."

His smile made her feel self-conscious, a micro feeling that was both instinctive and inconvenient because she needed to be switched on. It wasn't that she was hugely attracted to him, though he was attractive, but more that she knew too much and was struggling to reconcile what she suspected with someone she had always found agreeable and to a certain degree charismatic.

He lit his cigarette on the first attempt to release a strong and not unpleasant hit of a tobacco and they stood under the stone arches looking ahead at nothing in particular. The drizzle segued into heavier rain and the tapping of water on unknown surfaces gathering frequency and volume. He was an easy conversationalist but equally comfortable not speaking and dictated both states with ease.

"It was interesting to hear your speech about the new charity foundation," she said finally.

"Yeah, it's Carol's project really and she'll be doing the formal launch next month. I've got the business to keep me busy but whether it's the book or the new charity it's good for her to have a focus you know. Don't quote me on that though."

He sounded flippant, bored even, of the whole affair and she knew she was seeing something more authentic than in all the years of those careful, inhibited exchanges that took place when interviewed with his wife.

"Carolyn couldn't make it tonight then?" she asked curious.

"No. She's missed out though, it's not been a bad night as these sorts of events go, but I didn't think it would be your scene.

Isn't this all a bit fusty for you? Shouldn't you be hitting the clubs."

She knew she was being flattered and as their eyes locked, she was the first to look away and try to retain a more professional footing even though it would have been easy to play along if only to see where it went.

"The town twinning visit was good this year," she said awkwardly. It sounded clunky and at odds with the flow of conversation, but this was a rare one to one and she was unlikely to have the opportunity again.

"Oh, yeah?" he took a long a drag on his cigarette looking above.

"Yes, I always enjoy going – it was first time in 15 years since I was last there and it never changes. You've never been, have you?"

"Once."

"Oh really – with the town council?"

"Yes."

"Did you enjoy it?"

"I suppose so or as much as you can with these things. Can't really remember much about it."

And now he was looking at her more quizzically part curious and with an uncharacteristic coolness, unimpressed by the unexpected shift in the conversation but she ploughed on undeterred.

"When I was in the local church there, I came across this photo of a young boy - a kid who had gone missing from the village in 2000. The most bizarre thing was that it reminded me so much of Tom."

He stared at her without speaking.

"Sorry, I didn't mean to be tactless," she lied desperate for some sort of reaction. "It all just seemed the strangest coincidence."

"Coincidence? What do you mean?"

"Nothing really – just that – a coincidence – a boy that went missing in France so similar to Tom."

"Leah, where are you going with this?" he took another long drag and watched the plume hanging in the darkening air.

"Erm, nowhere really."

The journalist was disappointed in herself being passive and on the back foot, but it was the first time she had been on the receiving end of his assertiveness without the usual charm, and it unnerved her.

A surge of loud music cut through the silence as Gavin Smee appeared at the door viewing them quizzically.

"So, this is where everyone's hiding; Champagne toast and speeches are about to start, thought you'd want to know," he said.

"Thanks Gavin, I'll be in in a minute," said David efficiently as if dismissing an over enthusiastic waiter.

The town clerk went back inside leaving the two of them to resume an uncomfortable stare out, the unspoken heavy atmosphere of a line that had been crossed.

As the rain continued to fall, he flicked his cigarette on the ground.

"Anyway, it's good to see you making the best of things," he said eventually.

"Sorry?"

"Look, I don't think it's a big secret about you getting the sack in London – shit happens, not everyone is wired to thrive at the top tier of their profession; they bottle it, lose control but it can't be easy returning to their first job on the local rag either."

Her heart rate quickened.

"God how old were you then when you started on the Herald? – 18? 19?

"23."

"And what are you now?"

"None of your business," she snapped "Younger than you."

"While I'd say it's got to be about 38," he said eyes looking ahead as he made a mental calculation.

"You look younger I'll give you that, but you're still 38 and probably, knowing that place, on the same salary."

He let out a quick smirk that briefly distorted the familiar face she now viewed through an a very different lens.

"And it can't be easy to start again," he continued. "People speculating, not taking you seriously, not ideal in your game is when you need to be credible and convincing."

"Who doesn't take me seriously?" she asked, indignation and desperation rising.

"It doesn't matter Leah," he said as if appeasing an emotional child. "I just hear things about you, like the fact you're in therapy."

"So what?" she put both hands around her glass to stop it trembling. "It's hardly unusual or anything to be ashamed of."

"Yeah, perhaps you're right – it's best to get all the help you need. Is it helpful – therapy? I don't know anyone that's had it. I know we're all supposed to be a bit more progressive nowadays, but the reality is no one wants a loose cannon in the workplace being erratic with odd ideas and theories. People may know you're got issues, but it doesn't stop them judging does it and Maltham is so judgy isn't it."

The door opened again, and he was quick to react before Gavin could speak.

"Gavin, my friend, I'm coming," he said confidently putting an arm around the town clerk's shoulder as he headed inside, before turning back.

"Oh, if you'll excuse me Leah, it was nice talking to you."

She didn't respond.

"Are you coming in?" Gavin asked her.

"Yes, in a minute."

The door shut and it was a relief to be alone as she tried and failed to hold back tears willing herself to be stronger as her heart pounded, and the adrenalin surged through her body. She looked at the discarded cigarette thinking grimly that it was a fitting memento of their exchange.

* * *

David Steadman was trying to edge away from the milling tuxedos still wanting to talk to him. The dark cloud of a missing child should in many ways deter strangers from tongue tied small talk but not so with him; his confidence and charisma had always made feel both ease and in his thrall and as a local mover and shaker his attention was a highly sought after at this sort of event.

In the distance Gavin was gesturing towards him, but he could no longer go through the motions; his rictus grin on the verge of collapse; he needed to be alone.

"Sorry, Gavin," he said – gesturing to his phone– "I've just got an urgent call to make – I'll be right back."

"No worries - everything alright?"

No answer.

Past the lobby, the kitchens and waiting staff having a surreptitious cigarette, the man was moving too fast to be challenged which was just as well as he was in no mood to explain himself.

He finally reached the dark, unused wing of the building; a maze of locked conference rooms and guest accommodation with the music and laughter from the main hall now long gone. He flicked sweat away from his top lip as if swotting a fly and reached for his phone, forefinger hovering over the number in a rare moment of indecision grinding the back of his head into the wall and closing his eyes.

"It's just a random hunch, she's on the edge, its going nowhere, just a hunch, on the edge, nowhere.... bloody nowhere...."

He repeated it over and over again like a meditative mantra, but it wasn't working.

"Carolyn, it's me – look we might have a problem; Leah Chase – I was talking to her earlier and she only brought up Jacque Renard – she saw a bloody photo of him at the church when she was in Jean de Ruel on the town twinning visit."

Stunned silence, then finally.

"What did she say?"

"That the lad reminded her of Tom."

"Oh God. What else?"

"Just that - and she knows I was there in 2000. Look I've probably made it worse – I tried to, er... make out she's mad."

"Well, you're good at doing that aren't you," his wife retorted bitterly.

"Jesus Chris David – what did you do that for; we don't want to make an enemy of the local press – the Herald has been good to us over the years."

"Look, no one has found *any* connection in all this time, and I don't think some washed up reporter with a hunch is going to be any different, but we've got be careful."

"What do you mean – can't see the Maltham Herald stirring up any shit."

"Don't be dumb Caz; of course, they could stir up shit – that's what her lot do, and she has been a national journalist. Look, I think we should hold fire on the book promotion and anniversary stuff - we don't want to draw attention now that bitch is sniffing around for the wrong reasons."

"David, I'm not going to change any plans; that would seem

suspicious anyway; no, we have to carry on as we always do.... as normal. Do you hear me?"

"Normal??" he let out a snort and hung up.

* * *

Leah's key jabbed feebly at the door lock missing its target in her trembling hand as she swore loudly, shivering in the cool night air.

The last time she'd been thwarted by this most mundane of tasks it was down to some lapse of coordination in a happy, intoxicated state feeling daft but invincible as she kicked off her heels after a good night out in another life. Now only shock and indignation rendered her incompetent.

In the taxi from the castle, she had responded efficiently to enquiries about her night, mechanically concocting a version of an evening that sounded plausible and fun, the sort of night it should have been and almost was.

David Steadman had shown no such restraint, and their encounter had pierced her flimsy mental equilibrium, leaving her both paranoid and almost nostalgic for a return to her recent numb, insentient state.

With the door finally open she whipped her head around checking for any lurking attacker before slamming it shut dramatically. Heart racing, head pounding with no vices to smother the feelings, she leaned against it in the dark hallway and waited until her breathing steadied before turning on a side lamp as the familiar medley of brown furnishings of the large hallway materialised around her.

Somehow her childhood home had morphed into her adult one heavy with her parents' taste. They now lived in Spain for most of the year and she stayed here alone which meant it had got messier with mug stains pockmarking the hearth of the stone fireplace and faint cobwebs in the odd corner.

Yet she had little inclination to change it; by contrast to the attention she gave her personal style, she was largely ambivalent to her surroundings as long as they were comfortable and functional, and this detached bungalow in quiet, unremarkable cul-de-sac was undoubtedly that.

After changing into her pyjamas, she boiled the kettle and found a slab of parkin cake in the breadbin, carefully illuminating each portion of activity with the nearest side lights before switching it off after each task, still unable to cope with too much stimulus.

"Look, I don't think it's a big secret about you getting the sack in London – shit happens."

She brushed the dry sponge with the pad of her forefinger and got some butter from the fridge.

"People speculating, not taking you seriously...."

The spread absorbed instantly as she poured boiling water over two teabags in the mug.

"Loose cannon.... odd ideas"

Just the smallest splash of milk with the teabags left in.

"I don't know anyone else in therapy."

His words were on a loop in her head as hard and oppressive as tinnitus as she carried the mug and plate into a front room and flopped into her usual position at end of the comfiest couch.

Large, oak bookcases filled with her father's war and historical books lined one wall along with a cabinet of Yorkshire County cricket memorabilia. At the other end of the room was circular table, used annually for the Christmas day meal and for the rest of the time as a dumping ground for surplus magazines, clothes and unopened post. She pulled a blanket around her and ate her cake before removing the lid of a box that stayed under the coffee table.

She knew this was a bad idea as she stared ahead at a childhood photo. It was of her aged four at the zoo, looking like a boy and eating packet of crisps and it reminded her how she was often mistaken for a boy until she was about six.

She knew she should watch some escapist fluff on television to try and boost her mood but there was a perverse thrill to be had in wallowing in more judgement and condemnation and feeling angrier and superior to the many more stupid people that crossed her. She removed the first of four large binder folders, the contents of which documented the tit for tat fall outs and drama of her various employment history.

Someone in HR had been kept busy arranging the hundred or so pages into various sections with brightly coloured dividers, but she had also added her own leather bookmarks to pertinent sections.

"The role requires the person concerned to be both a strong team worker and to be office based. Your desire to work from home more often, and the fact that when in the office you tended to work individually, meant that the above requirement was not being met. Both myself, Kristen and Dianne Baggott discussed this issue with you on a number of occasions and sought to resolve it. However, prior to your longer-term absence on sick leave, your attendance record remained poor."

Dianne Baggott. She was struggling to remember who that was as she drank her tea. It always struck her how quickly these characters who at the time could be an all-consuming faded when you no longer shared the same sorry patch of carpet in the office. For the first time in as long as she could remember, she found herself considering if they still stalked the same floor of the building, clamped to the same old routine and superficial banter.

She flicked through more sections, the same phrases leaping

out on a loop: "not a team player" "spoken about many times", "number of warnings", disruptive, "disappointing".

"*Most alarming has been the significant deterioration (sic) in you're(sic) attitude over the last two weeks; sulking, door slamming and reluctance to stay late to complete a deadline. This has effected (sic) team moral(sic). I really feel I should add that of particular concern is the quality of your writing; to (sic) many sentences comprise of flowery long sentences.*"

The irony of being criticised by such an illiterate jobsworth amused her slightly but annoyed her more. The woman, Anne Wiley had been an HR bod, elevated to the lofty heights of communications director, more, Leah suspected by virtue of her longevity with the company and ability to brown nose than any particular skill or aptitude. Among many other flashpoints, they had repeatedly clashed over the editorial direction of a company magazine, a thin quarterly publication which justified both their employment, and no one read.

As such, cellophane-sealed copies in unopened boxes were dumped and rotated around the building, stacked in tall towers in the reception area or the stationary room where people would lean against them while waiting for the photocopier. On one occasion a pile was left in the corner of the staff car park under trees by the row of bins splattered with bird droppings, all of which had annoyed her then but now with the detachment of time had become grimly amusing.

And now she opened the remaining folder focused on the recent role that made for far less dispassionate amusement its contents still raw. The fifty plus pages of mostly email correspondence between herself and the newspaper editor, a linear narrative that read like tragic love story beginning with the mutually enthusiastic, polite exchanges, segueing into a power struggle and souring of relations before ending in the stiff legalise of disciplinary hearings and sacking. The end.

The final email that she was never meant to see and had printed out was found on her of former boss' computer and was an exchange between him and an insipid female colleague who had been nice to her face.

"The FAT BITCH writes one decent article and then wants it all her way – wants to work from home one day a week - cheek of it. I said no, then she mentioned the fact that you did of course - so why couldn't she etc etc, blah, blah, blah."

The reply from Jessica: "FAT BITCH! Oh my god, you're hilarious.... Maybe, the reason I work from home is because I have young kids, and she doesn't. Why's she so desperate to get out the office anyway – doing other work behind your back?"

"God knows - I think she'll walk out anyway... she's furious, looked at me like I'm something she trod in. If she doesn't go, we'll sack her anyway and I won't miss her moaning, talking shit and using up every mug in the kitchen. The sooner she's out the better."

Several hours later Leah woke on the couch, after a rare sleeping pill-free sleep, the email on the floor and her hand still in a troubled, tense claw. She sipped the dregs of her cold tea and turned on her side trying to ignore the birdsong and distant shrieks of the kids playing in the garden before school and wondered absently if they had come across the sanitary towel yet.

14

Maltham, England August 2017

Maltham Herald, Page 1

The future of Maltham Police station hangs on a knife edge this month as interested parties prepare to decide its fate at an extraordinary meeting of the council (Leah Chase reports).

As reported in the Herald last week, the Watts Road facility has come under growing scrutiny in the wake of an audit which revealed just 0.3 crimes had been reported weekly over the last year. Several developers have expressed interest in the site for affordable housing. It could mean that local residents will only have a hotline number to call to report a crime.

"This isn't the first time we've had to fight to keep this vital service," Jeffrey Lyons, Maltham (South) MP told the Herald yesterday (Tuesday).

"It feels rather like we're being penalised simply for being a community that isn't overrun with muggers and vandals, everyone I speak to about it this is rightly angry; they want and need the reassurance of a physical station and human presence, not a hotline."

Digested with a derisory sigh, Sergeant John Balchin tossed the paper aside, confident that this tatty '60s building would stay in situ, unfashionable and defiant amongst the encroaching, glossier infrastructure.

Yet, its barren interior with only a counter, empty vending machine and unpacked boxes hinted at some level of uncertainty. Posters promoting long expired events and urging vigilance towards modern slavery in nail bars and car washes were the only focal point on grey, stained walls.

Due in part, to the accumulated clutter of the long-established employee, the Sergeant's office tucked behind reception was a far homelier bolthole. On a quiet Tuesday lunchtime, in the adapted chair he needed to support an aggravated back, the 55-year-old was debating the merits of tinned tomato or vegetable soup. His eyes flitted between cans, held in stout hands, as he casually absorbing the ingredients list while Classic FM hummed in the background.

Decision made, he returned the can of tomato to the top drawer in his desk, broke off a bread roll from a batch of six from the supermarket and turned up Puccini, soaking up the melodrama that always took him from the hum drum to somewhere far more interesting that he'd never been and probably never would.

His body jerked as the reception buzzer sounded. It never used to have this effect, but the paucity of visitors meant this shrill noise had become as rare and intrusive as home callers interrupting his evening meal.

He emptied the can into his bowl, slapping the base of the tin urgently to probe its reluctant contents, an exertion which left him breathless. Chunks of cold carrot and peas and some unidentifiable grey lumps gathered pace, slopping into the bowl, and looking unappetising in its pre-cooked state. With the microwave set for two minutes, he hoped whoever it was could be dealt who quickly and pressed the start button optimistically.

"Good afternoon, how can I help?"

"Leah Chase, reporter from the Maltham Herald I have an appointment with DI Delaney."

She hadn't as it happened. It was an idea she had concocted on her way over during her usual detour past the Albanian car wash where attractive, dark-haired, olive-skinned, often topless young men scrubbed away at cars with intensity. Anxious to avoid being palmed off on someone junior she had wanted to give her visit a sense of planned officialdom by mentioning the one senior name she knew had been involved with the Tom Steadman case from the start.

The officer took in the well-dressed glamour and clear skin at odds with the many downtrodden characters that usually skulked through the station doors. He remained impassive though. Years of dealing with the unpredictable left him unphased by most of what came before him and wary of making any quick judgments.

"Well, that's strange because DI Delaney is out all day. Can I help"?

His accent still bore a trace of his Birmingham roots, and the journalist returned the once over he had given her. She absorbed the strained buttons around the stout middle, a ruddy, dry-looking complexion, pale eyes and thick thatch of sandy hair and eyebrows and felt reassured by his straightforward natural authority.

"I have some important new information regarding the Tom Steadman case. The boy who went missing from Maltham."

It hadn't been necessary to qualify. The officer, who was part of the original team nodded efficiently as she handed him the picture of Jacque Renard printed from her phone. He looked at it carefully before flipping over to translate the French inscription the on the back.

"Hmmm, he loved cats and dogs – did he?" He looked up at her puzzled.

"I found it behind some candles in the church in St Jean de Ruel, a small village in Southwest France. This boy went missing from there 17 years ago and has never been found, But I think he is Tom. I think that Jacque Renaud and Tom Steadman are the same person, she paused, quite enjoying the moment and the drama. "And he may have been abducted twice."

The distant ping of the microwave punctuated the moment as the implications hung in the air.

"Don't you think there's a strong look resemblance?" she said – hand gesturing to newspaper cutting of Tom Steadman, she laid across the counter.

His eyes darted around the material in front of him, and he raised an eyebrow in surprise, a small gesture the journalist seized on with enthusiasm.

"The eyes, the hair…. You know that Jean de Ruel is twinned with…"

"Twinned with Maltham, yes I know," he said calmly.

"And David Steadman – who claims to be Tom's father - was there when this boy went missing, he was there at exactly the same time– I have proof because it's all in the 2000 edition of the Maltham Herald; he was on the trip as the council's photographer – then just a few weeks later he's moved into the town with his wife and young child.

"And this child," she said, her long, thin finger prodding the image from the church he was still holding, "Has been missing in France since 2000 – the French media calls it The Red Shoe Case' – but it's never been solved – no body found."

It was a rambling spiel as if every element had to be unleashed in that minute to present as strong a case as possible, an intensity fuelled by her last encounter with David Steadman because avenging those who crossed her always motivated her more than anything else.

"*And* I know that David Steadman left the trip earlier than the others – said it was some sort of family emergency apparently."

"How do you know that?"

"The town clerk, Gavin Smee told me - he was on the same trip. Then there's the messages."

"Messages?"

"Left in a visitors' book in the village church from someone claiming to have witnessed the boy being followed by a man that day – I photographed most of them as well."

A small pile of printed off images was added to counter, the sergeant's dry looking hands picking them up and sifting through with interest.

He paused looking ahead, trying to compute this flurry of information that had pierced the most uneventful of days before making notes in the small black book that was always on his person. He took his time, checking a number of points, recording the details in bold, large handwriting.

"I know the case is closed ….". Leah added.

"Yes, there's no active lines of enquiry but the team and the cold case team at Surrey Police will always take a look a new intelligence and information. Would you mind waiting a moment?"

He disappeared and the journalist's eyes fell on an unfinished newspaper crossword.

Nine down: six letters: A desert rat that most commonly inhabits the desserts of North Africa.

She could hear his slow, measured tones talking to a colleague on the phone but wasn't able to catch what was being said.

Picking up a biro attached to the counter by string and Sellotape, she filled in the answer: Jerboa.

In the vending machine sat a solitary crumpled packet of skittles partially released from its plastic spiral and wedged against the side, she wondered how long it had been there and whether the colours of its contents were still lurid or had faded as she returned to the crossword.

Two down, six, three letters: A fruity superhero - some might say....

She scribbled the answer, Banana man, pressing firmly over the start of a wrong answer before returning the pen guiltily as Sergeant Balchin appeared.

"Right, Miss? Ms?"

"Miss"

"Miss Chase, thank you for coming; I'll share it all with my Inspector and we can update if anything comes of it."

For all her perceptiveness, the journalist couldn't fully ascertain if she was being humoured and tolerated and whether her appearance was simply a welcome distraction on a quiet, dreary day. Seargent Balchin gave very little away though in contrast to others with a certain impenetrable demeanour which could be tiresome, the woman found herself warming to his old school, measured manner.

"You weren't planning any kind of story on this were you? He asked. "You've only got a theory and no evidence, and I think you might just have the lawyers onto you."

The journalist momentarily thought of her editor - one of the very few newspaper men whose instinct was to back away from controversy and the big stories particular in the Autumn of his career that could threaten the quiet, simple life he craved until retirement.

On his watch she knew there would be no plans to publish anything at this stage though she didn't communicate this, leaving the situation ambiguous in the hope that the threat of publicity could encourage a more open dialogue with the police team.

Not that the sergeant seemed phased either way as his eyes fell on the completed crossword.

"I've been wrestling with that all morning," he smiled. "If you need any updates in the meantime your best port of call is through the press office."

Leah groaned inwardly at the thought of Nicola Prescott but managed a small smile as she made her way out. Beyond the four walls of the police station people were going about their business on this unremarkable afternoon. Such was the intensity of her focus it was as if she had forgotten there was a world outside and while it was hardly a sprawling metropolis, the hordes of people traipsing around lost in their activities momentarily surprised her.

The lightest of drizzle had petered out before it got going, as unsure what to do with itself as she was, as she watched the endless energy of some boys in the skate park, crashing down ramps, attempting ever more elaborate jumps and spins, rising fast and unscathed from falls with the invincibility and stamina of youth.

Hyped but drained, a restless lethargy was brewing inside her like the aftermath of a panic attack when the surge of adrenaline was over, but the effects still lingered in the body. On auto pilot she headed to one of her regular lunch haunts, phone in hand poised to update her editor.

* * *

Having watched the journalist head towards the high street and disappear from view the Sergeant put down the paper he was pretending to read and returned to his office. He shut the door and leant against it, releasing the tension in his neck before pacing the room, unsure what to do first.

He settled on retrieving the soup from the microwave and transferring it to his mug for easier, faster consumption and sat at his desk. The movement induced a pang of lower back pain and the usual accompanying groan as he impatiently tapped his keypad to rouse his computer from sleep mode. He accessed the system he needed and sat forward expectantly as files documenting every facet of the Tom Steadman inquiry began to materialise, hundreds of little lemon squares rows belying the scope of the drama within.

First, he clicked on the case review files, the first dated 28 days after Tom Steadman was reported missing, then those that came at three, six- and twelve-month intervals before progressing to annual reports.

Devoid of a breakthrough they had become little more than predictable, anodyne templates that only merited a quick scan. Of greater interest were the witness statements and the more offbeat material that could transport him back to that hot summer when his then 40- year-old self still had much to prove. He peered at one of his earliest reports annotated with his own barely legible scribbles, one of which referenced the fabric, chainmail helmet, which had been part of the boy's jubilee costume and lay scrunched and abandoned by the Steadman's doorstep.

It was largely familiar material, but with both the lapse of time and impetus of new information, it acquired more poignancy infused with a broader sense of nostalgia. Former colleagues – the big personalities that had loomed large in the station during those busier days now retired or expired were briefly resurrected by the nuances and turn of phrase in their notes and comments that the Sergeant read with interest.

Credible witness statements remained as powerful and

precious as ever. He signed deeply as he re-read these fleeting observations and tutted as he was reminded how often some unlucky quirk of the faulty surveillance camera had put paid to a more successful follow up.

Another gulp of soup as he lingered on an image of Tom Steadman and fellow pupils captured at the start of their jubilee procession. Taken by a teacher, it revealed the usual mix of compliance and distraction amongst a group of young children some beaming others looking elsewhere.

It had been taken about an hour before the boy disappeared. Like footage of a president on the cusp of assassination or the imminent death of its star casting a shadow over their final film, the poignancy came from the timescale. Here, the missing boy seemed so conspicuous, the only one whose hand is held by a teacher, under duress, her arm fully stretched as he pulls away with infantile defiance. The end of one of his trainers is digging into the middle of his other shoe, a plastic sword is held high in his other hand. His character looks big and stands out, as does the distinctive outfit.

"How come barely any bugger remembered seeing this," he said to himself flatly

He read through more witness accounts that recalled the school procession snaking around the town, part of the fabric of the day along with the floats and the muffled beat of the town band and paused on the final line in that section. Key witness: deceased.

He was so immersed in the task that by the time he finished and closed the files some two hours had passed leaving him feeling the usual mix of sadness, frustration, failure and guilt, though tinged now with a little hope.

He typed in the Red Shoe Case – and sat back taking in the images of the dense woodland in France and officers stood by a lone red shoe.

* * *

"Table for one"?

Leah nodded unsmiling. She was a regular face here but maintained a formal efficiency with the staff. She suspected they viewed her permanently solitary status as weird and antisocial, and she had no interest in being humoured by strangers with an eye on a tip.

Not that dining alone bothered her. What seemed to be an unfathomable oddity for some was one of her reassuring routines in testing times. As a junior reporter seconded to the Maltham Herald's dullest satellite office, lunching at a hotel nearby became a much-needed reprieve from the repetitious musings and nagging of the sixty-something chief reporter she was holed up with.

"Have you been sitting on your own again in the Georgian?" The woman would ask, face swollen from her latest health scare, the stench from her lunchbox consuming the airless portacabin that constituted an office. "What on earth for?"

"I know, it's odd when it's so much nicer to eat in here," she would reply sarcastically watching the woman shake her head with the usual incredulity she showed towards any preference or behaviour that didn't chime exactly with her own.

"I don't know, what a strange girl you are Leah, such a strange, strange girl."

Towards the end of this penance, the younger woman had taken to simply raising a middle finger behind her colleague's fat back and keeping it there as she waited for her computer to fire up. It was a gesture that unbeknown to Leah, the woman could see reflected in her computer screen but oddly, in a rare show of restraint never mentioned.

With her usual table taken, Leah was shown to one the size

of a domino wedged between two large sprawling table, noisy families.

The place was full of these people, something she only tolerated because of the quality of the burgers and keen price which meant she could eat well for around £11 including coffee, in short, the kind of value unheard of in this town.

She ordered her usual Cajun burger with extra relish and triple cooked sweet potato fries and tap water, put the menu back and took in the familiar sights, pained looking offspring being bribed and cajoled to eat a chip while the next bloated plate arrived ready to be spilt and played with. In truth, she came here, partly to be annoyed because she knew sharing space with these sorts of people would irritate her and she took some warped pleasure in feeling this way, feeling something, along with a sense of superiority and relief over not being them.

* * *

Her editor's reaction was as expected, a flutter of interest mixed in with his natural reticence towards any sort of a scandal as they sat in his office – the various cuttings and photos of Jacque Renard laid out on his desk.

"We can't report anything based on a hunch, we will need to follow the proper channels and go through the press office," he said. "We're not a tabloid, we have to do things by the book, err on the side of caution or we could potentially compromise a very big case."

It was advice she already knew and had expected, but in reality, it was an approach informed more by his nervy disposition than any moral high ground. Caution had become a convenient excuse for inertia and a general reluctance to tackle anything much beyond the comfort zone of planning disputes traffic gripes and the odd Golden Wedding.

It irritated her but she understood. The man was long past the need to prove himself- his role had segued more into one of an efficient caretaker, increasingly kowtowing to local politics and a managerial agenda than the newshound of his younger days.

Increasingly his office door would be locked after lunch - the explanation that he needed "to crack on" without interruptions not always convincing on a slow news day. The wider team gossiped about him slacking off and secretly listening to the cricket and on one occasion Leah heard faint snoring coming from inside as did his secretary though neither woman mentioned out of loyalty.

Yet contrary to her boss' assumption, Leah's real motivation was to establish the truth and keep riding a momentum that had given her some needed purpose and distraction rather than any rash reporting that could put them in contempt of court.

"You've got to admit it's pretty compelling though; what about David Steadman's reaction to me at the Partridge dinner? Why would he be so rude and defensive if there was nothing in it."

The man shook his head wearily.

"Well, assume this is all pie in the sky; it's a sensitive subject for a start and if there's an insinuation being made that's way off the mark of course he's going to be prickly."

"No this was more, I dunno, more sinister somehow, like a sort of pent-up fury of someone finally being challenged."

"What was he saying anyway? You said he was being rude."

"Shitty comments about me being in therapy."

"How does he know about that?"

"God, knows."

"You know my feelings on the Steadmans; taking to one side what has or hasn't really happened, they always struck me as pair of nouveau riche chancers, flashy and with a fair old degree of entitlement."

The pair sat in silence on either side of his desk with the relative comfort of two people who had seen the other at their best and worst, were resigned to the fact that neither were likely to change and aware an alternative could be far worse.

"I would like to go back to Jean de Ruel though as soon as possible," she said finally

"What on earth for"

"To do some digging of course – speak to the police there, maybe try and chase relatives of Jacque Renard; it's not that long ago – his family can't be that old can they?"

"Assuming they're still in the area."

"Anyway, you are not on a national now," he said archly. "You can't expect extra little jaunts over there to be authorised on the Herald's budget."

She looked at him without saying anything, the usual approach she adopted until she got the answer she wanted. It was a surprisingly simple but effective tactic that encouraged people to appease her just to fill the awkward silence. Peter especially was always vulnerable to persuasion and secretly welcomed her newfound enthusiasm though he didn't want to encourage her too much.

"Let me think about it. Perhaps a few days won't break the bank, but if I agree, *and* that's a big if," he said pausing for effect and pointing a finger as if remonstrating with a child.

"We will have to keep this just between ourselves or everyone will be wanting little trips to the seaside. And Dave Garland will have to cover Carolyn Steadman's charity launch at the castle but then perhaps that's not a bad thing for you to have a bit of distance from them."

She had forgotten about the event but agreed with her editor that it probably was for the best.

15

St Jean de Ruel, France August 2017

Jean Phillipe Gaubert hadn't had a drink for a few days, yet alcohol still seeped from his pores stubbornly resistant to the medley of aftershave and spearmint he used to try and mask it.

He had been oblivious to this in the way that those who emit odours from their person usually are enlightened only after a visit from his ex-wife, who he didn't like anymore but whose judgement still carried weight. It left him self-conscious that an affliction he thought was well hidden could be common knowledge where he lived, worked and rarely strayed from.

Unable to give up alcohol completely he had taken to keeping more of distance from others where he could, though in his small papeterie this was impossible. Here, customers mulled over the purchase of expensive fountain pens at his counter testing nibs and asking advice. It was an intimate service experience he had always enjoyed but was now spoilt by paranoia as he lit more joss sticks and scented candles which everyone commented on when they came in and he wished they wouldn't.

In the church of Saint Jean du Ruel where he was a regular presence, it was far easier to loiter in the shadows. Today, as always, he sat on the back pew close to the figurine of Saint Antoine which held a white Lilly and the baby Jesus. He thought as he always did, that a male saint carrying a child looked unusual and scanned the familiar setting with a deep sigh, unbuttoning his coat.

Usually, the place was solemn, dark and silent, but next month's impending itinerary of the harvest and chestnut festivals had galvanised the church volunteers who had temporarily taken over the space. Prayer and contemplation were temporarily on hold amid the preparations as flowers were replaced and the group of two men and three women in their sixties pondered the placement of a bowl of chestnuts, a task which consumed them for several minutes.

Well acquainted with the rhythm of church life, he had anticipated this delay and came prepared. A flask of coffee and a ham sandwich, half concealed in his bag next to him was positioned carefully so he could break off small lumps of bread and eat discreetly, avoiding the risk of being caught with a baguette in his mouth and treating the place like a café.

He slowly worked his way through it as the scene before him became absorbing as things do with no other stimulus, as he watched the group's gesticulations and flicked crumbs from the small tapestry kneeling cushions and snatched sips of coffee.

By now, the bowl of chestnuts had been repositioned several times around the chancel with little tweaks made to the angle having negligible effect. A consensus over the location finally arrived as he finished his lunch and wiped buttery hands down his trousers, while the group surveyed their efforts in a small semi-circle before dispersing to gather bags and belongings.

Sensing the possibility of unwanted conversation, he quickly knelt down, eyes shut, and hands clasped on the wooden ledge in front of him with the group's chatter hushing respectfully as they passed before the door opened and closed. It occurred to him while he was down there that perhaps he should pray for real, his permanent state of guilt and unease always in need of an outlet. A minute or so later he slowly got to his feet, his bony knees feeling the impact of hard floor and walked to the bookcase and took the latest visitors' book from the second shelf before returning to the pew. He removed a fountain pen from his bag and flicked impatiently through to a new page where he wrote his latest message in bold, purple ink, conveying the usual sentiment.

"I saw him following the boy along the Rue de Stade, he thought no one had noticed him; but I did."

As always, he read a few of the responses to his last entry, disappointed by the vitriol of strangers accusing him of attention-seeking, and demanding he reveal his identity. Pen lid clicked back in place he returned the book to the bookcase and went over to the candle rack to replace the drying posey with a fresh one by the photograph of Jacque Renard. Throughout this he had been oblivious to the barely audible whir of the surveillance camera positioned high above the pipe organ behind him recording his every move.

16

St Jean de Ruel, France, September 2017

Leah Chase sat in Le Midi du Nuit's petit salon enjoying a post dinner coffee. As usual it came on the silver platter with a generous jug of steamed milk and homemade chocolates so texturally perfect, that the first cool, dense bite was one of her favourite tastes on earth.

She had returned to the latest edition of Paris Match, trying to get the rub on a saga involving an ageing rockstar, whose dishevelled plight wandering shoeless with heavy eye bags near his former childhood home been captured by the paparazzi's long lens and spread across six pages.

This space was now fully hers after bidding Bon Nuit to a Parisian couple who usually came in here for a drink at the same time before retiring at around 10pm. Affluent and well-preserved the wife would sit on the edge of the sofa with clasped hands and very straight back, drinking mint tea and never touched her chocolates.

It was the kind of feminine restraint that all looked a lot of effort to the journalist, who after they left would finish the untouched chocolates before sinking into the leather armchair with another magazine.

The pair were typical of the hotel's remaining guests, no longer with young children and tethered to school timetables and busy jobs, intent on wringing out the last dregs of summer over long dinners and coastal walks. Peak season's churn of activity had transitioned to the more subdued vibe of early September, and everyone seemed to have more time.

The hotel dog, a self-sufficient terrier usually left to its own devices was now indulged like a baby while the patronne's focus could migrate to more peripheral matters like removing stray leaves from the pool.

Without the usual requirements of the town twinning committee schedule, Leah drove her own more lax agenda.

Most days she ventured further afield, often to a quiet, rugged, beach lined with pastel beach huts as small and uniform as monopoly houses. Empty and locked to the elements, they were backdropped by cliffs with scalloped edges like singed paper and surrounded by rushes that swayed rhythmically in the keen wind.

Along the beach front were a couple of cafes whose unremarkable exteriors betrayed the quality of the food inside. Packed with regulars who never needed to be anywhere else, their extrovert interactions played out in the background as she ate moules a la crème and watched the walkers trickle in from the coastal path to weigh up the menu options chalked outside.

The next day, she returned to the church which in common with her other regular haunts here felt more subdued and appeared more ordinary without high summer's strong light casting multi coloured reflections through the stained-glass windows.

Incensed with the usual mix of musk and age, she discovered

that Jacque Renard's photograph had disappeared from the candle rack along with the usual posey of black roses bar a few dried out petals, edges curled like stale crisps. She walked over to the bookcase which no longer held the visitors' books. In common with much in life, change was rarely welcome and the absence of both had left her disappointed and deflated as she sat in her usual position in the back pew and returned Peter's call.

"Hi, it's Leah, just got you message. How are you?"

"Not bad, what about you? Up to much?"

"I'm in Jean Du Ruel church. The photo of Jacque Renard and the visitor's books with the anonymous messages aren't here anymore."

"Well, I suppose the French police will have taken them; their cold case team has reopened the Red Shoe case."

"Bloody hell."

"Anyway, you shouldn't be on your phone in the church. I do hope there's no one else there."

"Only God."

"If anyone comes in, you'll have to take it outside, won't you?"

"Yes, I will," she appeased wearily, with a roll of the eyes well-used to humouring his degree in the obvious instructions. "Tell me everything."

"Well, I don't know that much but I got a *strictly* off the record update from Sergeant Balchin telling me that the Millau cold case unit were taking a fresh look at the case following some new lines of enquiry. Oh, and some woman called Nicky has been trying to get hold of you."

"Nicky? Nicky who?"

"Rosling, Rasling? Something like that; says, she's – wait for it – a *former* friend of Carolyn Steadman and wants to talk to you and you only. Dave Garland spoke to her briefly and took her number, I'll give it to you. Now have you got a pen ready?"

She scribbled down the mobile.

"So where does that leave us in terms of what we can report?"

"In bloody no man's land." He sighed heavily. "There's no confirmed link to the Steadmans yet and certainly nothing we can go ahead and publish."

"But they obviously think there's something worth looking at and the fact I started it all off means we should be all over it."

"Look, you know the drill; it's too early and there's no substance. You can make yourself useful though while you're out there; get yourself down to Millau police station and ask to speak to an Inspector Bertaud - she's leading the investigation; you probably won't get much but it's worth a try."

The conversation limped along with a sense of something else pending and unsaid in spite of the flurry of information.

He told her about the unseasonal weather in Maltham, humid and very cloudy – almost an Indian Summer apparently, then the unwelcome re-appearance of charity collectors lining the high street pestering him to sign up to a direct debit donation whenever he left the office. It was mildly amusing but at odds with his usual efficiency on the phone; she knew something was afoot but didn't pre empt the bombshell that finally came.

"Leah, I told the rest of the newsroom this morning, so now is probably a good time to let you know that I'll be leaving the Herald next month, I'm finally retiring."

Silence.

"I've been thinking about it for a while, I'm not getting any younger," he expanded filling the pause.

"But I thought you were still enjoying it – particular with all this Tom Steadman business... we're right on the cusp of breaking the Herald's biggest ever story."

Embarrassingly, she realised she was close to tears.

"I know, but I'm nearly 70 don't forget and there's other things to do. My wife wants to travel, take more holidays while we still can, I want to see more of the grandkids, and I do get very tired.

"I hate people's other halves," she thought to herself.

He sounded very tired.

"I remember you saying that retirement and holidays were for people with boring jobs that have to have their fortnight in the sun to make life bearable."

"I know I did, but I need to be less selfish, and I have been over the years. The Herald takes up so much of my time. Anyway, when I say travel, we're probably talking a barge up the Norfolk broads not The Ganges…. it looks like management are considering a former Daily Mail sports editor to replace me – Robbie McQueen – after a quieter life, away from London I suppose," he went on. "From Scotland originally, also writes golf books."

Leah's head tipped back a little and she briefly closed her eyes. When she opened them, she discovered the ceiling was also heavily embellished, a circle of angels orbited a depiction of Jesus carved into the stone without any additional colour.

"Leah? Are you still there?"

In many ways, the news shouldn't have been the shock it was. Peter's retirement had been mooted for some time but in common with the many things the journalist didn't want to face, she hadn't allowed the possibility to register. Without her most sympathetic ally, all she could see was a bleak, depressing future in an office dominated by a morose Dave Garland and a disapproving Sue Lansford.

The perks she had slowly cultivated since her return – trips into town on the pre-text of some meeting that were never questioned, the under-discussion request to work from home more often, a mooted office of her own – all of which would all evaporate with the arrival of a new dispassionate, unforgiving broom who in time honoured fashion would reverse any favourable decisions and view her more critically.

Not that she would convey any of this and how much she would miss him.

"So, is this Robbie a shoe-in then?" she asked blankly.

"Well, it's looking that way. The management see it has a bit of a coup, getting a former Daily Mail editor."

"Suppose they would. Though he's not a *real* editor, is he? It's the journalistic equivalent of a PE teacher."

She could hear Peter sigh disappointedly.

"Do try and keep an open mind."

"Well, I suppose there's not much more to say right now," she said, an edge of petulance creeping in to induce a guilt trip. "I'll let you know how it goes at the police station."

"Yes, you do that I'd been keen to know what they say, have you…

"Someone's just come in. I better go." she lied

"Yes, ok, Leah, bye for now, Take care."

She tossed the phone into her bag and pressed her back hard into the pew's wooden headrest. Only the new phone number belonging to the mysterious Nicky contact scribbled on the back of her medication packet stirred some interest and distraction amid the doom.

Rolling her neck from side to side, her eyes fell on the gold Jesus figurine which today was positioned in the vestry. Eventually she got up and walked listlessly down the left side of the church past the series of uniform stone arches and the saint figurines on the wall. Zipping up her leather jacket against the growing chill as she reached the confession box, which with its short, flimsy curtain appeared to offer an inadequate screen to any of the revelations disclosed within.

This was the darkest corner of the church and judging by the piles of dust and discarded knick knacks, one that was neglected by both congregation and cleaner. Beyond the confession box within a tiny, designated alcove stood a figurine of Saint Therese that could easily gone unnoticed and which the journalist didn't recall seeing before.

She was dressed in her dark brown Carmelite robes with one arm holding a doll-size depiction of Jesus on the cross and the other outstretched, an open palm, in which the photograph of Jacque Renard she had discovered on the previous trip along with a single black rose had been placed.

Perhaps it was more of a response to Peter's news which had left her feeling vulnerable, but the discovery sparked some emotion in the journalist and for the second time in five minutes she fought back tears. The image trembled a little in her hand as she ran a finger along the familiar creases and turned it over to discover a new comment had been added in the same purple scrawl of the visitor book messages on the back. It translated as:

"The truth is almost here".

Back at the hotel that evening Leah got talking to an English couple after the wife, Brenda, complimented her outfit, over aperitifs in the Petit Salon and seemed to be interested in her job as a journalist as people often were.

As someone always susceptible to flattery, Leah had begun to see the women more favourably than the provincial dullard she would have otherwise dismissed her as and she took them up on their offer to join them for dinner.

The pair were retired teachers and easy company used to holding court and pontificating on topics of little substance. Their conversation was peppered with house values, car upgrades, their grown-up sons doing well for themselves in IT and teaching respectively, thinly disguised disapproval of said offspring's spouses and the granddaughter's scholarship to a local private school whose IQ put in the top percentile of children her age in the country. It could have been spectacularly tedious and in many ways was, but after a day which had passed with barely any conversation beyond ordering lunch Leah was ready for a little social interaction.

Plus, Peter's retirement news had unsettled her making her more receptive to an undemanding, easy distraction and the perks of an upgraded menu that came with their treat.

Things became far more interesting when she discovered the pair had been visiting the region for the last 20 years – always in July in the long summer holidays they'd enjoyed as teachers and in September since retirement.

She asked them if they had heard about the Red Shoe case which seemed to pique their interest, and she went up to her room to fetch her case folder full of print outs and press cuttings. Laid out on their table amongst the discarded shells from their lobster sea platter, the picture of Jacque Renard attracted some sympathetic recognition from the hotel's patron whose lack of English, limited any meaningful contribution.

The English couple thought the child looked familiar but didn't know if that was because they had seen him in the French press or if was down to another reason. It was a response that could have ended there unsatisfactory but shortly after the crepes arrived dripping in Grand Marnier and the wine flowed, Don recalled the return ferry journey in 2000 speaking to a man with a toddler in the restaurant queue.

"There was a delay as the chef went off to refill the trays of lasagne. We were standing there a bit bored and hungry and this miserable looking child in front of us was staring up at us so hard we felt quite sorry for him, he looked shattered and, oh god, so fed up, so we asked the man what his name was just as something to say really."

Leah sipped her wine, as her heart rate quickened.

"And he paused for ages, like it was the most difficult question," Brenda interrupted

"It was bizarre - like he didn't have a clue."

"That's rather an exaggeration Bren – it was probably only a few seconds."

"A few seconds, a few minutes what does it matter; it was long enough to be bloody odd wasn't it? And you were the one that commented on it afterwards – how many parents do you know who seem unsure what their child's name is."

"Anyway, that kid did look a bit like this – don't you reckon Bren?" said Don, his gold signet ring brushing over the cutting of Jacque Renard.

"What about the man he was with? Does this ring a bell? "Asked Leah holding up an image of David Steadman on her phone.

Don tilted his head as he weighed up the small headshot in front him.

"Oh, now you're asking. I think he was quite tall probably mid-30s at the time but as for anything else it's a blur."

"I really can't remember either," replied his wife, turning to Leah. "You don't think it's the same child, do you?"

"Oh, who knows, probably unlikely," said Leah closing the folder now ready to dampen down the spark she'd ignited. She knew only too well that not retaining information was as important as being able to extract what you needed from others and that it would be easy to let the talk segue into idle gossip that could potentially threaten the future exclusive.

Anyway, anecdote relayed it seemed the couple were ready to change the topic.

"And how you finding the Grand Marnier?"

Leah nodded her approval, watching the pair write down the details of the wine so they could stock up on at the local Carrefour oblivious to the potential bombshell they had delivered.

In common with many people who have lived in the same area for too long little piqued their curiosity beyond their immediate stomping ground and grandchildren. The saga of a missing child that happened elsewhere and sometime ago was no exception just another diversion over a pleasant dinner. In some ways Leah was relieved by their apathy, which spared any expectation to get drawn into detail which right now she didn't have energy or inclination to share.

The three returned to their puddings and collective murmurs of approval.

"So, what name did he give eventually?" asked the journalist trying to sound casual

"Oh, now you're asking," Brenda said downing her dessert wine.

"Tom," said the husband matter of factly.

"How on earth did you remember that darling?

"Only because it was my father's name, and I remember thinking was a good, solid choice."

While the mix of medication and morish peach bellinis left the journalist feeling dazed she was still alert to the couple's potential value in the future.

"We should swop details and stay in touch," she said, eventually as the three of them folded their serviettes with varying degrees of attention. "I'm always meaning to get over to Norfolk as well."

The words sounded odd and alien even though they had come from her mouth.

"Absolutely," said Brenda, a small smile forming as she wrote their address and phone number on the back of a leaflet.

"And you'd be very welcome to stay with us."

"Yes, I'd like that. Sounds good."

17

Maltham, England, September 2017

"Firstly, I'd like to thank you all for coming to the launch of The Tom Steadman foundation. The event has taken a lot of planning and been a real labour of love, so it feels very special to finally share this with you all tonight."

Carolyn Steadman scanned the tables that formed a loose horseshoe around the castle's wooden hall pausing with a smile as her voice coach recommended. The idea was to build rapport with the audience, but applied a little too mechanically, the delay felt clumsy and laboured as if she was waiting for an applause that didn't come. Eventually, distant coughs percolated as she returned to the notes written by her husband.

With an abrasive tone and tendency to over emphasise many of the words, public oration didn't come naturally to her, though her physical presence and the context of the event more than compensated. Swathed in a clinging, gold Herve Ledger dress, her dark hair loose and blow dried she was, as always, the photogenic face of a tragedy, a potent mix that had seen the event sell-out fast and explained that intangible buzz of interest and anticipation from those gathered for their latest fix of the mystery.

"Now, when our son Tom went missing 15 years ago, life for my husband David and I as we knew it was officially over. Of course, we have never given up hope that he will be found safe and well and that one day there will be some resolution to all of this, but we are also realistic and know life must go on. It's why in the last year I have had to face some big questions: mainly, I suppose, what is my real purpose now?

She looked out again across at the floor for too long as if expecting someone in the audience to provide an answer before returning to her notes.

"I came to the conclusion that the best thing I can do is be productive to not only keep my son's name alive but channel what has happened and the platform I have for good causes. Later on, you will be hearing in more detail from some of the project partners about how we will be supporting families with missing children as well as raising funds for causes that have a connection with Tom."

In the dim light, the Maltham Herald's chief sub editor Dave Garland peered hard at his watch, debating whether to go for a cigarette before catching the disapproving eye of the woman opposite and returning his focus to the stage. Used to the more solitary routine of porn and a takeaway this black-tie event with its explosion of social formalities and loud, well-to-do vivacious people was proving to be an assault on his sense and he already felt drained and exhausted.

Tonight, his behaviour and habits, tolerated by colleagues, fell under the more critical eye of strangers though there had been some perks. He had especially enjoyed the free hospitality with all the abandon of someone not paying, requesting more wine, second helpings of roast duck and both dessert options reasoning to the bemused waiter, that the portion was likely to be only a mouthful anyway.

As Carolyn left the stage, he distractedly joined in the applause a few seconds late and looked at his watch again as those around him resumed their conversations. He surveyed these exchanges blankly as if watching a dull television programme that couldn't be switched off, entirely untroubled by his exclusion and feeling bored rather than awkward.

Attempts had been made to include him by those on his table, but he didn't really do what he termed 'prattling' or 'talking shit' instead offering monosyllabic answers or in the case of a rare topic that interested him, talking over the other person slowly and avoiding eye contact all at odds with the light, conversational froth expected.

Eyeing a young waitress, he downed the rest of his wine before retrieving a stubby bookies biro from his trouser pocket. In view of his recent promotion, he was resigned to carrying out his duties albeit half-heartedly and scrawled the gist of Carolyn's speech down and got a quote from a couple at his table. As he predicted, they were delighted to be there and to support such a good cause and were great admirers of Mrs Steadman, citing her strength of character and how resilient she was, especially in view of what she had been through because such adversity can so often take its toll on people's looks.

Off the record they felt the event's £95 a head cost was a little steep, a comment the sub editor pounced on, and they instantly regretted saying. Over the next ten minutes they would say three more times that they did not want to be quoted on that and if they had his complete assurance that this would not go in the paper. The sub editor found a perverse enjoyment in not doing quite enough to allay their concerns and seeing how this trivial matter had begun to escalate and compromise their enjoyment as he watched their pensive faces and conspiratorial discussions with a derisory smirk.

He looked at his scribbles on his page with a puzzled expression. He had never bothered to a learn shorthand, instead devising his own version that saw some words shortened or replaced with various symbols which made sense to him but no one else and meant, to his editor's and other colleagues' irritation, that his notes could never be shared which was ultimately how he liked it; people should do their own work and reporting he'd say in defence, not everything is a team effort.

Yet as the slow swell of booze starting to numb his brain and mark the stirrings of a state that could flip between morosity and jet-black dark humour in seconds even he was struggling to understand his notes.

At the top table sat the usual dignitaries along with Carolyn Steadman, all of whom he needed to get quotes from. He considered briefly inventing some soundbites, but the depressing reality was that at the age of 58, he was too worried about getting into trouble with his boss to risk it. He would speak to them properly, but not before a much-needed fag break and he rose from his seat, grabbing two petit fours and putting them in the pocket of his hired tuxedo before slipping out of a side door into the castle grounds.

* * *

In the brief lull that followed the speeches Carolyn Steadman had begun to ponder what she really doing here. Ostensibly, according to her speech and the worthy but repetitive conversations that followed it was to honour Tom. Forming this charity in his name was to lend her experience to supporting others with missing children; but she wasn't convinced.

Whether in therapy, dealing with the press or the public she had become ever more used to following a script and behaving in a way that was suggested or expected by those around her and tonight was no exception. She was in many ways a strong person but lacked initiative and relied on others for ideas and inspiration usually her husband who had been keen for her to find an outlet and had suggested charity work.

The unsatisfactory conclusion she came to as she watched her mineral water being refilled and mentally calculated the calories in the two petit fours served by a gum-chewing waiter was that she had no idea. Was it just a chance to get dressed up and be centre of attention? Another distraction to take her mind off things, a reason to get out of bed?

She was inherently sociable, a party girl who missed the fun of her younger days but all of this with its formal and polite conviviality and measured sympathy was little substitute.

She was surrounded by strangers who thought that after 15 years of press coverage of a local saga that had backdropped their lives, they knew her as opposed to the curated version they were presented with. As always, this resulted in an odd, careful dynamic that smothered her natural inclination to laugh and be uncomplicated, as if publicly at least, she was only meant to existed in a state of more sensible, stoic sadness.

If there was any kind of clarity in that moment as she made one petit four last three bites it was the realisation that she was sick of talking about Tom and being defined by the affair. It was a bitter irony given the purpose of the event as she registered more polite smiles from the couple opposite and wearily returned the gesture.

Sighing deeply, Carolyn dipped down to one side of her seat and retrieved her clutch bag which held her lipstick, purse, toothbrush and toothpaste and left the main hall, through the lobby filled with dark historical portraits and large display of her new book, *Tom Steadman: A Mother's Child*, on her way to the toilets.

After checking each cubicle was empty, she entered and locked the one furthest from the main door and opened her clutch, taking out her toothbrush and inserting the handle end deep down her throat to bring up everything she had just eaten. She punched the flush button and brushed her teeth at the sink reapplying her lip-gloss and a little lipliner an automatedly efficient process that took just a couple of minutes.

As always, her reflection confirmed a certain disconnect between the outwardly groomed appearance and the torment inside – smooth, tanned skin and almond eyes fronting an inflamed stomach, acidity in her throat and raging turmoil of her head. The permanent smack of fluoride in her mouth would clash as it always did with wine or whatever else she was to consume yet the sensation was always reassuring in its confirmation of a routine completed, a purge ticked off from a daily quota as she ran her tongue around her teeth.

Her phone vibrated in her clutch, and she read and deleted a text from her husband wishing her luck. It had been sent just 10 minutes earlier and felt like an afterthought adding to her irritation that he wasn't there with her. Her fingers stroked the tiny perfume bottle pendant hanging from her neck, her fortieth birthday present from him. She removed the stopper and spritzed CK One at arm's length before walking into the citrus scent hanging in the air. It was her final preparatory step that began decades ago as part of the preening ritual in nightclub toilets and she was hit by a wave of sad nostalgia of the days she danced on podiums.

Walking through the corridor she returned a few smiles from other guests. In the distant lobby, her name was being mentioned by someone with a loud, grating voice and she waited outside until whoever was talking had left before entering and arranging her hair onto one side in front of the mirror.

The neat pyramid of books arranged at start of the evening was now a messy heap as she noted the well-thumbed but unpurchased copies with a small derisory shake of the head, relieved when someone approached her asking to sign a copy.

Now at the entrance of the main hall she paused. Framed by an ornate white archway she appeared like a giant artwork as people turned to look at her. She tried to secure her clutch. It was strangely consuming task due to an unreliable vintage clasp and when she looked up, she drew breath at the sight of a two uniformed police officer and a suited detective colleague talking to castle staff near her table.

The development was so unexpected and so unwelcome it took a minute to compute as if she was viewing something in hyper reality. She could see the mayor and two other people from her table also getting involved, looking puzzled and gesticulating, while everyone in their orbit turned around in all directions looking for someone, that she knew to be her.

A strange hot sensation swilled around her body, weakening her legs. In spite of the strongest instinct to run and to keep running, she remained rooted to the spot as she looked bleakly ahead, consumed with the heavy, oppressive dread, of being trapped and no longer in control, fate sealed with the only option left simply to watch it all to play out. A fear that had always been inside intermittently smothered by routine, distraction, money and vices could no longer be contained and in the moment, as she realised with such clarity how naive and pointless all the pretence and tactics she had deployed over the years, had been, how it was only ever going to delay the inevitable that, like death, was always going to come.

Now she could hear the flurry of good-natured assistance from unsuspecting guests, directing the officers towards her.

"Oh, there she is, just over there, in the archway. Is everything all right officer?"

The officers didn't reply. They strode briskly and purposefully towards her, stern and unsympathetic faces eradicating any remaining flicker of doubt over their intentions as they got closer and her heart pounded so hard and she tried hard not to shake. Tables of turning heads tracked their progress, as some people stood up for a better view, as the detective strode a little ahead while the uniformed officer responded conspiratorially to muffled noise emitted from his radio. Strong, capable arms she noticed as her panicked mind lept to wild, thoughts of trying to resist arrest and break free, under normal circumstances these arms would have been simply attractive with their defined muscle and smattering of tattoos. And now they were there eye to eye, solid, determined, business like and impenetrable.

"Carolyn Steadman, I'm arresting you in connection with the abduction of Jacque Renard. You do not have to say anything. Anything you do say may be given in evidence."

"Oh God, no. Please don't handcuff me, not here in front of everyone; it's the launch of my son…, my missing son's charity."

"But it may harm your defence if you do not mention when questioned something which you later rely on in court."

"What about my husband? I need to speak to my husband."

"Your husband is also under arrest and has been taken to another station. We won't handcuff you, but you will need to come with us now."

Her shaking hands had failed to close her clutch bag and as she walked through the throng of tables, faced scorched red and burning, her toothbrush fell out landing by the detective's size 11s.

All eyes were now fixed on the random object, with no one moving or speaking before the detective, who had introduced himself as Inspector Delaney, bent down and handed it back to her. She snatched it in her trembling hand and the small party was on the move again, her sandwiched between the officers, dwarfed by their tall frames and bulk of their stab vests, like a boxer surrounded by his entourage on his way to the ring.

Earlier in the evening her presence had been commanding and visible from every part of the room and it still was for all the wrong reasons, shrunk to a slither of pale, gold shimmer, like a small flame, tiny and vulnerable struggling to stay intact against the wind. Puzzled murmurs swelling around them as they passed table after table on this excruciating long walk, the pairings of gawping waiting staff who had materialised to watch the drama as Carolyn kept her head down and eyes fixed on the marble floor, trying to steady her breathing until she got outside.

"Carolyn are you ok – is it Tom? Has there been an update- have they found him".

Oh, there's been an update all right she thought grimly ignoring all comments and questions.

In a life lived in a state of almost constant dissatisfaction and anxiety she was used to having to find small moments of respite during episodes of otherwise abject misery and here it was the simple relief of being outside and finally escaping the stares and scrutiny.

Light rain was falling and bringing with it that fresh scent and gentle rhythmic tapping as her thin frame shivered in her cocktail dress awaiting the latest instruction from her captors. Her cashmere pashmina, a present from her husband had been left at her table but she has no energy to mention it. In the police car window, her white, gaunt reflection shocked her, a stark reminder that trauma penetrates the gloss however well applied and on auto pilot she started to rearrange her hair into a side ponytail.

"My pashmina is still inside the castle."

It was barely audible and of little interest to the policeman, who with a firm hand steered her into the back seat.

A flutter of open-mouthed indignation and the door slammed, and she started to cry.

* * *

Dave Garland's curiosity had got the better of him as he walked across the castle's immaculate lawn towards a small mound shrouded in a white sheet surrounded by rose bushes. Fag switched to his weaker hand, he lifted part of the damp sheet cautiously to uncover the bottom half of a bronze sculpture of a child wearing T-bar shoes, knee high socks and shorts pulling it all the one to reveal a familiar face, eyed fixed on a cat held in small hands.

Inscribed on the base were the following words:

To mark the official launch of the Tom Steadman foundation, founded by his mother Carolyn Steadman to support the ongoing search for missing children.

"Bet that cost a bit," said Dave Garland to himself absently dropping sheet back in its place and grinding the tip of loafer onto his finished fag but. No doubt we'll have to troop back out here later for the big reveal; I'll try to remember to look surprised."

The man was used to talking to himself. He looked up the black sky and sighed. He had been outside for about fifteen minutes and knew he ought to return but he was struggling with the motivation and lingered.

With a daily routine that flitted only between his bedsit, the office and the pub, the man was rarely in any kind of attractive garden these days and it had been a surprising bonus inhaling the sweet scent that had grown headier and more pungent in the wet.

In fact, the appealing and ordered aesthetic had almost sparked some rare compliance as he toyed with picking up his cigarette but and putting it in a nearby bin, but he eventually decided against it. Resigned to his duties, he folded his arms against the rising chill, and made his way to the entrance, head turned by a passing police car carrying an occupant on the backseat who he couldn't see in the rain. As he retrieved his notebook and pen and found a blank page, he wondered grimly how he was going to fill it.

18

St Jean de Ruel, France, September 2017

Retrieved from its steel time capsule, and displayed in its plastic evidence bag a red T-bar shoe – around five inches long - took centre stage in a grey, hot meeting room at the police station, five miles from St Jean de Ruel.

It was a faded version of its once vivid scarlet hue and several scuffs were visible, testament to the stone and gravel that had punctured Jacque Renard's small, unsteady steps on route to the Foret de Bois on that hot July afternoon, 17 years ago.

Smudges of dried soil flecked an outer edge bordered by intricate maroon stitching, while a slightly slacker, elongated third hole indicated where the buckle's prong routinely pierced the thin strap. Still visible on the insole, was the logo of a now defunct quality children outfitters and the number five shoe size of a two-year-old Jacque Renard.

In spite of its tender size or perhaps because of it, the object held a curious power, arousing some rare and unexpected emotion within the two UK senior detectives, Sergeant Balchin and Detective Inspector Delaney. Not that this would have been apparent from their outwardly impassive appearance as they took their seats and cups of coffee and eyed the sprawling display before them.

Over 17 years' worth of files, papers and press coverage on the case, pale and crisped by age and musty from storage, were laid out on the large grey table bringing the waft of an unoccupied house to an already airless room.

The 200 plus editions of Le Sud-Midi – the main regional publication sat in its own designated and pile. National press, mainly Paris Match and the Sunday supplements were in three more bundles. Here, the boy's familiar stare shared covers with various French celebrity misdemeanours and royalty, a darker contrast to the fluffier, indiscretions and scandals around him that once mattered, but unlike him, were long forgotten.

Collectively, it seemed the press had exhausted most angles and theories, a scrutiny that had ebbed and flowed and generated its own sub plots and players depending on the agenda of who was writing the narrative. Commentators with right leaning sensibilities had tended to pass the greatest judgement on the boy's young, single mother, speculating on how and why a toddler had been left in the care of other children, able to roam near a wolf-ridden wood in the first place, a negligence, which in their eyes rendered the actual consequences less relevant.

For others it was a dependable narrative to revisit as part of a broader attack on police incompetence or the impact of budget cuts or an excuse to whip up extended family feuds that had predictably come to the surface amid publicity.

Born just 10 years before the boy's disappearance, the French officer, Detective Constable Jean Clemenceau, sat on the other side of the table fiddling excessively with these print towers, shuffling and adjusting, running his thumbs down the edges, flicking off dust and trying to do the same with stains that were going nowhere.

By virtue of his position in the room, he was the only beneficiary of a faint breeze that rolled in intermittently from the small back window. Head down, he was rather absorbed in this task, as if entirely oblivious to his audience of two which in the absence of any other stimulus was fixed on this repetitious activity almost as if in a trance.

Occasionally, the two British officers would make weary eye contact wih a mutual roll of the eye and pull at their restrictive collar and ties before returning their gaze to his busy fingers.

Heads tilted, eyes narrowed, both attempted every now and then to read the upside-down headlines and blurbs in French while trying to dodge the sun glare with ineffectual tweaks to their position.

With no offer forthcoming, Balchin toyed with simply asking to be handed a few copies to read properly but the room was so silent that even he felt uncharacteristically awkward and self-conscious. It was as if the volume button had been muted and any utterance however light he would try to keep his intonation, would feel as intrusive and unwelcome as the sudden smashing of glass.

Jacque Renard was the room's fourth occupant, wherever the sergeant looked, being pushed on a swing or stroking the black cat on his lap, absorbed and frozen in time and oblivious to the drama that enveloped him

He wiped the back of his head that was now damp with sweat and tilted it from side to side to stretch an aching neck brought on by the tension of a long drive on unfamiliar roads. It was a rare flicker of action that prompted a quick glance and muted smile from the French officer before his focus returned to the bundles.

Mainly confined to his desk, Balchin wasn't so used to long journeys these days or indeed, leaving the UK at all, especially for work. While the old thrill of reviving a dormant case with its unfinished business was stirring inside, this turn of events was also taking it out of him.

As the sweat poured, and his waistband continued to feel as restrictive as a straitjacket he thought for the first time that he should perhaps listen to his doctor's advice and take better care of himself and get some bigger trousers.

Inspector Delaney was feeling equally stifled as he crossed his long wiry legs and arms tightly. The silence which had in fact lasted for three minutes and 20 seconds seemed interminable and with as little French as his colleague and nothing that extended to the complexities of this long-running cold case it was easier to keep quiet for now. It seemed an unspoken agreement existed between the trio to suspend any attempts at conversation until the French inspector arrived, so they remained like nervy strangers in a dentist's waiting room.

When the door eventually opened, it was abrupt and roused everyone from their silent lethargy. For the two British officers it was a jolt heightened by the woman's appearance firmly at odds with their expectations of the 'ball-breaker' Delaney had confidently predicted on the journey over.

Inspector Cecile Bertrand was young, at least for someone in such a senior role, slim, highly groomed with thick, blow-dried hair and an elegant beige suit, doused in Dior Rose perfume which left a scented footprint around the room and injection of feminine energy that pierced the mood and dynamic.

Sergeant Balchin downed the last dregs of his coffee and looked up expectantly. Having resented being kept waiting he was low on the patience he usually had to muster for social pleasantries and keen to get on with things.

In perfect English with an accent mellowed by education in

the US and UK, the French inspector began the case update with more detail on the new eyewitness statement taken from Jean Gaubert owner of Papeterie Gaubert.

"He had been trying to sleep off his latest drinking binge in the flat above his shop but kept waking up and remembers seeing Jacque Renard – a boy who came into his shop regularly with his mother walking past on the Rue de Stade," she said

"Having shown him a photo of David Steadman, Gaubert believes that it is the same man he saw walking some way behind the boy that day – a significance lost on him at the time, but of course later on he realised...."

"Which is why he spent all this time leaving silly little cryptic clues in the church?" interrupted Inspector Delaney with a disapproving shake of the head.

"Well, yes, his way of saying what he knew without revealing his identity. It's clear he has felt very guilty and troubled over not doing more and feared the judgement probably. If we hadn't put the surveillance in the church, he may never have been identified because no one had ever caught him leaving those messages before – he was obviously very careful which is why it's been such a long and puzzling local mystery."

"Why didn't he just go to the bloody police station sooner," added Balchin folding his arms and stretching his legs out in a bid to alleviate his cramp.

"Perhaps, he thought no one would take him seriously," she answered with an animated shoulder shrug before quickly scanning her phone, curiosity piqued by something on the screen.

"In view of the circumstances and the state he was in at the time – an alcoholic really struggling to function he feared his contribution wouldn't be very credible."

The woman's elongated pronunciation of David into Da – veede had started to grate on the Sergeant as did her casual dictating of proceedings.

His colleague, Delaney, was her equal in rank and the older man had anticipated a more equitable exchange of intelligence and updates, perhaps even some polite inquiry as to how the actual arrest of the Steadmans back in the UK had panned out rather than playing pupils to her teacher.

He thought with some bitterness, that for a woman who had needed heavy persuasion from her UK counterparts to reopen the case she had the smug swagger of an individual whose own foresight and initiative had made the breakthrough alone. The impetus for establishing the identity of the mystery writer in the church had come from their lead on David Steadman and there seemed to be little in the way of gratitude and acknowledgment.

He sighed deeply and tried to catch his colleague's eye as a beige folder come out of her briefcase its contents swiftly distributed. In their hands were the now familiar images of Jacque Renard/Tom Steadman, as part of a report entitled Morphological Comparison. This contained the findings of the forensic artist who had been tasked with trying to ascertain if Jacque and Tom, were indeed the same person.

As requested, they turned to page three and absorbed a series of overlaid images of the boys faces at age two and four and a breakdown of the comparison of facial features set out in bullet points.

"So, if we start with the consistencies that have been identified by the artist between the two individuals who in this report are referred to as Jacque Renard and Male X," said Inspector Bertrand.

She was perched on the edge of the central table, holding her papers in the style of newsreader or lecturer trying to appear more informal.

"The configuration of their features was found to be similar for the upper portion of their faces; the positioning of the eyes, the width and height of nose and snub tip and round nostril shape."

She paused as the information was digested, walking over to the window, attention caught by a heavily pregnant dog, its head slumped, pacing up and down over an overgrown piece of grass either trying to alleviate its discomfort or find a suitable birthing spot.

"We also have a rounded lower lip and some interesting skin details that are not always clear in photos," she said turning back to face them.

"You will see that a small scar has been identified in both images just above the right eyebrow, the kind of detail which can go a long way in providing support for a conclusion."

The officers peered closer. It was as if, under this forensic scrutiny, they were seeing the face for the first time, though with neither man prone to waffle nor big gestures, both settled for muted murmurs as their heads stayed bowed consuming the details.

"Please turn to page five," continued the Inspector. "The artist has identified some

inconsistencies between the faces, though on balance it seems, they can be largely attributed to the age difference between them."

A long, pained howl could be heard from outside which everyone ignored.

"As a two-year-old here, the facial contours of Jacque Renard are very full, the bridge of the nose is flat, the eyes look large and round, and the hair is soft and fine. By contrast, the eyes of the four-year-old Male X are more elongated and less round, the upper and lower jaw have enlarged and widened and though the nose is still small and button-like the bridge has started to form and the chin has begun to take shape. The hair has thickened and the lower section of Male

X's face is more elongated than that of two-year old Jacque Renaud."

A pause followed as if she was waiting for slow pupils to catch up and when he looked up DI

Delaney realised the woman was looking straight at him.

"The eyebrows also look pretty different," he offered feeling under pressure to say something.

"Yes, they do, don't they?" She pounced on the contribution in the manner of a teacher coaxing a reluctant student.

"Do you get a prize?" his sergeant mumbled.

The French inspector continued: "But the artist believes this can be attributed to the positioning of the head in relation to the camera and the difference in expression."

And now all eyes fell on the final page and summary that said while the analysis could not be used as conclusive evidence of identity there was strong support to the assertion that Male X and Jacque Renard were the same person.

Impressed with the detail, DI Delaney sat back in his chair, uncrossed his legs and smiled at his French counterpart who, unlike the man next to him, he was warming to.

Sergeant Balchin made the right noises but thought to himself it was an odd focus to start this briefing with. If he had been leading this, he would have gone in with the money shot: the revelation that the DNA sourced from the abandoned red shoe was a match to hairs retrieved from Tom Steadman's hairbrush; far more compelling than putting so much steer on something that while useful could never be definitive.

Still, he had only been pounding the beat when she was at primary school, what the hell did he know. As he downed the last dregs of his coffee, he couldn't resist piercing the upbeat mood.

"So, we know we're dealing with the same boy; a boy that was snatched by David Steadman when he was over here in

2000 who he and wife then passed off as his own kid when they returned to England. What none of this clears up is what the hell happened to him in 2002 – the Steadmans didn't take him twice did they? They both had alibis, so who took the poor bugger the second time?"

It was deflating summation and as he looked at the blank faces, taking a small satisfaction from a temporarily muted French Inspector. For the time being at least there was still no answer.

* * *

The journalist had felt buoyed by her brief call with the mysterious Nicky. Not surprisingly the woman sounded wary and tense confirming she had some "unbelievable" medical evidence on Carol ynSteadman but to disclose it would be a confidentiality breach that put her job at risk.

As such, she would have to remain anonymous and could only meet in person rather than sharing details on the phone, as how could she be sure she wasn't being recorded?

In Leah's experience, such caution was often disproportionate to the value of the information being disclosed. However in this instance she suspected a bombshell that would put her back at the epicentre of this unfolding drama.

It would give her visit to the French police both point and purpose and ammunition to bat away any reticence from a team she knew would be reluctant to share information with a reporter - even the one that had warmed up their case.

She went to the station on the penultimate day of the trip. In common with many government buildings in France, it had a grandiose, elegant, aesthetic disproportionate to the modest town it sat in. Sat in the foyer area optimistically holding her Dictaphone and notebook, she eyed the comings and goings of staff and visitors up and down a central marble staircase noting the contrast to the grey, tatty block that constituted Maltham's counterpart.

When DI Bertrand finally emerged clad in leather jodhpurs and silk shirt, her expression set the tone for the brief exchange that followed, a masterclass in impenetrable efficiency.

The woman had been interrupted and wanted to get back to whatever it was she was doing, a sigh of repressed exasperation, as the journalist rattled off how her theory had reignited the iconic case and made clear her expectation of an exclusive update.

"Have you confirmed that the French missing boy is Tom Steadman?" Leah asked, but the question sounded tired and lacking conviction, like it wasn't expecting an answer and hung feebly in the air.

"Can I introduce you to Detective Constable Clemenceau," said Bertrand, relieved to see her junior colleague coming towards them and being able to bat the reporter away.

In a hot shoebox of a meeting room, Clemenceau took ten minutes to tell Leah what she already knew. Sensing the futility, the journalist produced the photograph of the latest purple note she had found in the church on the back of Jacque Renard's picture.

The officer viewed it with a neutral expression and confirmed they now had a key eyewitness helping them with their enquiries whose identity would not be shared. She left feeling flat and offended and began to question why that was. It had been easy to convince herself that her main motivation in this case all along was justice and answers, but it was also evident that she wanted personal glory and the recognition and reward both as personal and professional validation after a troubled time.

The last day passed more listlessly with the sense of expectation and promise that had sustained her all week now gone, compounded by Peter's news. She made a final visit to the church before dinner lighting a candle and noticing that the photo of Jacque Renard had been returned to the clasp of St Therese. It was here, in the uncomplicated silence that she was reminded she only knew half the story anyway.

19

England, September 2017

During her brief stint as a national journalist, Leah could read her articles anywhere, a reach and visibility that brought a needed buzz and mitigated much of what was wrong in her life.

Her bylines in the Maltham Herald once had the same effect because in an irony lost on her at the age of 23, the town had been as much the centre of her world as it was for the local stalwarts whose parochial concerns and narrow horizons she would joke about with colleagues.

Yet life and experience had shifted expectations and 96 miles into a 100-mile journey home from the ferry port, the local paper's limited scope had never seemed so acute. Only now on the edge of Maltham town centre could she finally pull into a garage that still stocked copies of the Maltham Herald to read Dave Garland's hatchet job of the Steadman's arrest, which she knew wouldn't merit the anticipation that had stirred during the long, dull journey.

A blast of Nina Simone cut out with the car engine, and she

looked blankly at the empty forecourt thinking how far away Southern France seemed, despite the garlic aftertaste of last night's bouillabaisse still lingering.

That morning, she had sat in *Le Chat Noir* courtyard mustering a certain conviviality with the familiar faces whose visit had coincided with her own. Now, as she watched a driver emerge from his parked HGV on the layby and head into woodland, she was ready to return to more anonymous interactions.

She got out the car, trying to coax legs heavy and tired from too much inactivity back to life. It wasn't especially cold, but the weary discomfort of a day's travel meant her bare arms fell the chill as she crossed the forecourt passing a car emitting the low thud of R&B from its open window.

Mumbled comments from two cap-wearing teens sat inside were ignored. She waited for the automatic doors to open, a rising impatience and sense of expectation inside of her.

Inside, LED lighting framing the chiller cabinets and ceiling affronted her tired, dry eyes. The scene was quiet, bright and depressing; a cashier absorbed with a scratch card, another staff member crouched down replenishing boxes of Battenburg cakes on the shelf.

The front page of that week's Herald was dominated by the write up of the Patridge Dinner and a large picture of Carolyn, looking attractive and tiny in a clinging gold dress stood between Vince Dunkett and the usual medley of tuxedos and taffetas all holding copies of her new book, *A Mother's Story.*

Her pose with one leg forward was in the vein of a Miss World contestant, her face tipped to its best angle, a smile showing uniform, whitened teeth,

Casting a critical eye, the journalist registered Dave Garland's by-line in a larger font size than standard with a tut and shake of the head, a triviality that irritated her more than it should have.

This year's sell-out Patridge Dinner at Maltham Castle also marked the launch of a charity foundation in honour of missing Maltham school boy Tom Steadman (Dave Garland reports).

Around 150 guests including the Mayor of Maltham, Vince Dunkett and Lady Beryl Tride heard from Tom's mother Carolyn who shared memories of Tom, who hasn't been seen since June 2002, and her new charity which aims to support the families and friends left behind when a loved one goes missing.

She's got some bloody nerve thought the journalist transfixed as she read the full report including the details of a menu that included truffle roast potatoes and the unveiling of a statue of Tom with no mention of any arrest.

On page four came the crime round up. In between a shoplifting charge and drunk driving sat the following announcement

A 56-year-old man and 47-year-old woman from Maltham have been arrested in connection with an abduction of a child from France 17 years ago.

Due to sensitives and the complexity of the case no more details are available at this time.

A spokesman for Maltham Town Police confirmed the man and woman have been bailed and enquiries continue.

With a copy under her arm, she moved quickly around the aisles grabbing a packet of scampi fries and a can of coke as well a jar of manuka honey and £10 bottle of olive oil – both of which she didn't want to pay for. She bypassed the cashier fixed on the comings and goings on the forecourt and used the self-service till, scanning only the crisps and paper. Her finger jabbed at the option confirming she didn't want a ten pence bag before plucking one from a pile hanging from a small hook.

"She don't change much, does she?"

Leah jolted a little and looked up to see an older female

cashier with a copy of the paper, gesturing towards the picture of Carolyn.

"Carolyn Steadman?"

"Yeah, never looks any older which is weird innit when you think what's happened. Think she'd look more stressed. Reckon she's had something done?"

"Probably." The journalist smiled weakly, gathering her haul and headed towards the automatic door staring blankly ahead as she waited to be released.

Back in the car she put her bag in the footwell and took out the coke and crisps. The combination was a throwback to her old post night out snack and its nostalgic taste was comforting as she flicked through the rest of the paper with a mild interest.

There was a double page spread of the month's farmers market as well as a story slamming the growing intrusiveness of charity collectors in the high street. It centred around the experience of a local businessman who claimed on a typical day he would be accosted up to four times "often with backchat" when he failed to comply. The man was also a good friend of her editor and tended to be a reliable source to parrot Peter's pet grievances.

She tossed the copy on the passenger seat screwed up the crisp packet and shoved it into the drink holder and reapplied her lip gloss on auto pilot. From her bag she removed her folder stuffed with notes and cuttings pertaining to the case. It now included the contact details from the Norfolk couple and Carolyn's former friend Nicky Risling who she had planned to meet tomorrow.

It was reassurance that she had new material to work with, which as far as she knew was exclusive to her and would be kept to herself for the time being as she thought about her next career move.

Peter's retirement news had been a sobering reminder that

his editorship had not only made her return to the Herald possible in the first place but also more or less bearable ever since. Any motivation or commitment she had mustered over the last few months was out of loyalty to him and with him gone, she knew she would no longer have a future there.

Her involvement and insights with the case far exceeded the parameters of the Maltham Herald; there would be no better opportunity with which to relaunch her career.

She would continue for the next few weeks until Peter's last day while planning her comeback based around her definitive account of how she helped solve the Red Shoe case securing an exclusive with a national newspaper and then hand her notice in.

Maltham, England, June 2002

Maltham Herald, Page 1, June 8th ,2002
FINAL preparations are underway for Maltham's Golden Jubilee celebrations tomorrow (Friday) with large crowds expected to gather in the town centre for the street party and carnival.

Volunteers have been working around the clock to ensure a day of a packed events to celebrate Her Majesty Queen Elizabeth's 50 years on the throne with barriers already erected along the high street to contain the expected crowds.

On the eve of the event the Head of Maltham Town Council Gareth Grey told the Herald: "Once again, Maltham has shown what it can achieve when the community comes together. I would like to take this opportunity to acknowledge the support of town clerk Gavin Smee, (correct) and the hard- work of the communication team, especially Nick Denser and Jessica Humphries assisted by Ros Cowley who have selflessly committed many hours to ensuring the day will be the success everyone is expecting."

Turn to page five for Friday's schedule of events in full.

. . .

"What about Ros then?

The council's assistant director of communications looked at her boss Nick expectantly with an impish grin.

"What about her?"

"Well shouldn't we invite her."

"Seriously? Can you see her clubbing, or even pubbing for that matter; it would be like taking your mum out for the night. Don't even think about it Jess, I'm warning you."

"Yeah, but the joke is that she's younger than both of us," said his colleague pleased at how the response she had anticipated was playing out.

"And she'll be disappointed if she's left out – she loves you... it could be her one chance to pounce."

The man, perched on the end of Ros's unmanned desk rolled his eyes and fiddled absently with the lid of one of her pens. It was pink and plastic and formed in the shape of a cat with a furry coat which he held up with a questioning smirk and shake of the head.

"Haven't you noticed?" the woman continued. "Making you all those coffees, fetching the papers, quite the little PA as well as a press officer."

"Not so little, though is she."

The pair laughed as Jess, approximately half the weight of Ros, playfully slapped the back of her colleague's head in mock reprimand thoroughly enjoying the impromptu bitch session.

"To be fair," he said, "The girl doesn't make a bad coffee, I'll give her that or at least she normally does - and it's a very important skill for a press officer these days, if she'd made shit coffee she would have been out on her arse by now because those bloody press releases aren't getting any better."

"Well, as long as you're kept in caffeine that's the main thing; anyway, what do you mean she normally does?

"Eh?"

"You said she *normally* makes a good drink – what's gone wrong, I'm intrigued?"

"Oh, I didn't tell you, did I? She only added some powdered cinnamon that she got from the garage next door to my coffee, couldn't bloody believe it – apparently it was because she'd heard me saying how good the spiced coffees in Morocco were on holiday."

More laughter with Jessica throwing her head back dramatically as she was prone to doing in these situations.

"So, are you're telling me that she bought it especially?"

"Yeah – so I got a mugful of Nescafe with a dollop of a cinnamon powder floating on the surface like shit on a pond and when I drank it, it caught my throat, so I started coughing and couldn't stop – just before that employee engagement meeting as well. Needless to say, she was very, very apologetic, fetching me water, shitting herself actually."

More laughter.

"Bloody hell... I bet you thought you were back in Marrakech after sampling that delight .... Bless her she's got a serious crush mate."

"Don't even joke about it!"

The communication chief yawned and stood up stretching his arms above his head and taking the opportunity to expose some of his newly acquired abdominal definition as his shirt came untucked.

"Anyway, I will see you, young lady, later. We're meeting the others at The Bear for 8pm, bye for now."

"See you later. Looking forward to beer night."

Ros who had heard the entirety of this exchange in the

nearby kitchen was waiting for one or preferably both to leave so she could fetch her coffee mug, which she always rinsed before she went home.

Feeling the effects of a day hunched over the computer she tilted her neck from side to side and stretched her left-hand splaying fingers that had gripped the computer mouse for too long and needed coaxing back to life. While she remembered she opened the cupboard and retrieved the pot of cinnamon powder to take home and use when she next made rock buns.

Eventually the office door opened and she heard her boss's brisk steps sounding down the corridor and more loud confident laughter and brief indecipherable exchanges with the colleagues he encountered on his way out of the premises. From the window she watched him strut across the car park, pleased with himself as ever, his head turned by a young girl who had been doing work experience in another department.

When he got to his white BMW, he shouted over to her inviting her to the Bear pub at 8 pm that evening if she was around adding that it was going to 'get messy'.

His car backed out of the parking space fast with a flourish, convertible roof slowly retracting as he put on his sunglasses turning up some music, she didn't recognise but was Eminem. He seemed to do everything very quickly she noticed, and she recalled overhearing him on the phone to a friend, saying that walking fast made him appear more dynamic and therefore, younger which was why most of his colleagues assumed he was around 38 when he was in fact 42.

She looked at her watch. It was now 5.45 pm and she wasn't sure if Jessica had already left but she couldn't wait any longer as she wanted to get home. The door opened just as she was about to turn the handle.

"Oh, Hi Ros, thought you'd gone ages ago," said Jessica, a lipglossed rictus grin attempting to mask any discomfort she might be feeling.

"I've been in a meeting downstairs."

"Oh right, actually I glad I bumped into you – just wanted to check you'll be ok to come in early tomorrow?"

Ros nodded without questioning.

"Nick is working from home tonight, no doubt 'til late, bless him, to finalise plans for tomorrow's jubilee stuff so he'll be in a bit later in the morning and I have to drop the little people off at 10 am for their school event so won't be here 'till about 10.30ish, so, it would be brilliant to know you are here manning the fort for us. Bless you."

A small stroke of her arm.

"Yep, that's fine, no worries."

Her colleague paused on her way out turning to the other woman.

"Up to much this evening?" asked Jess going through the motions.

Ros's usual routine ensconced on the sofa watching soaps flickered through her mind and she felt no need to embellish it.

"Not really, a long soak and just some TV I think"

"You're making me soooooo jealous now, that sounds so chilled - the joys of not being tied down with kids and having all the time in the world to do what you want. See you tomorrow honey."

"Bye Jessica."

The press officer replaced the lid on her cat pen to stop it drying out and took the mug from her desk disappointed at how stained it had become in spite of her diligence. It had been one of several new items she bought when she was offered the role along with a pleather briefcase and stationery. She rinsed it in the kitchen sink under the hot water, scrubbing harder and harder while monitoring Jessica who was now walking across the car park, her progress hindered a little by her high heels and fitted pencil skirt.

The heat of the water made her wince, but she didn't move her hands.

21

Maltham, England June 2002

As always Tom Steadman tried to drink his cereal directly from the bowl before being reminded to use a spoon.

Dressed as a St George's Knight for his school's Jubilee celebration the small, stocky figure perched on a stool at the matching steel breakfast bar was as inert as Carolyn Steadman was frantic.

Dressed for the gym, in her cropped vest and leggings, the woman who had just turned 30, tossed keys and a protein bar into a plush holdall while gulping multiple pills and supplements pausing only to stifle a gag reflex. At the whiteboard she scribbled several instructions and reminders for the collective paid help: notes about flower orders and an organic cleaning fluid preference.

She left the room and walked into her home office, still yet to be properly used despite a lengthy and costly refurbishment. A new laptop sat expectantly on a desk carved from a slab of Italian marble bearing two small yucca plants, boxes for filing and some Smythson stationary, a set of five notebooks in descending sizes embossed with her initials, a birthday present from her husband.

Sometime yesterday she had picked the smallest book and written on the first blank page the date and the words *To Do* which she underlined before her attention was diverted elsewhere and it remained on top of this pyramid of stationary expectantly.

She replaced the lid on the marker pen and walked back into the kitchen twisting it around in her fingers like a majorette twirling a mini baton, watching the boy swirl the last of his milk with a chubby forefinger turning the white a chocolate brown. She tried to keep calm. It was simple alchemy that never failed to absorb him but irritated her, the routine, the repetition, the duration, messy, chocolate fingers. She sighed deeply. Attempts to replace the cereal with one that didn't offer the same time-consuming novelty had sparked a tantrum so intense that she had no wish to repeat it.

Only 8.30 am. Today was not even a regular school day. Jubilee events meant a 10 am start while her own plans were as fluid as ever, yet she was so agitated. She resented school themed days, and with it the changes to her routine and the tedious requirements to make cakes and costumes at short notice.

"Considering the bloody fees we pay, I think the school should provide a costume," she had said to her husband the night before, who murmured his agreement but with the detachment of someone who wouldn't be personally inconvenienced by any of it.

It was, she argued typical of the kind of demands which were only likely to increase and as such strengthened the case for hiring a nanny an idea, she found herself increasingly fixed on as the magic bullet that would alleviate her stress and improve her low mood and her life generally.

Today, she would catch up with the usual faces at the gym, a routine that usually expanded to coffees, a sauna, probably a treatment and ended with a long lunch somewhere serving exorbitantly- priced and small portioned Caesar salads.

It was hardly the most demanding of schedules, yet she had the wired energy of someone guilty and about to appear in court. For the last month or so she was conscious of the steady, audible throb of her heartbeat, whether active or still, in bed or the bath, the physical response of a racing, frantic mind and rushing cortisol. She had started to crave cigarettes, a recently resurrected habit that remained a useful appetite suppressant and alternative to making herself sick when her salivary glands had swollen, and her face and neck started to look puffy.

Smoking wouldn't help her complexion, but she was in no state to be too disciplined and while she could control her food portions and pretty much everyone and everything around her, she had her limits.

She grabbed the packet of Marlborough lights hidden under a copy of Cosmopolitan in a fruit bowl full of solid silver apples and unlocked the kitchen door that led to the patio. Her hand trembled slightly as she took a long, first drag but the effects felt as good as ever surging through her body as she watched the smoke corrupting the fresh air heavy with birdsong and a plane leave its white, plumy trail across the skyscape.

The heat was there already, heavy with promise of another stifling day. She closed her eyes and tipped her head back enjoying the warmth on her face and her mind wandered from the here and now as it tended to in these rare moments of peace.

As usual, memories of her five-year-old self and her father at the dog track started to stir. It was the place they would go most weekends and the one of the most defining memories of her childhood with its machismo, noise and energy, the air reeking of hot dogs and aftershave and where, buoyed by their mutual enthusiasm, their effortless, organic bond was most acute.

She turned to look at the small figure at the counter still messing around with his cereal, a wave of tension swooping through her body as she took other long, satisfying drag and looked back up the sky once again, faced flushed with the dry heat.

And now she remembered the faint little creases that had started to form around the corner of her eyes and that she had planned to cut down on her time in the sun and stop smoking. She stubbed out the cigarette and opened the doors, hands clapping fast in a bid to chivvy up the small figure still immersed in his breakfast. He looked up from his bowl briefly before resuming his stirring and then drinking it from the bowl.

* * *

Valerie Hobson was always early these days. Any diversion from her usual home-based routine triggered a level of planning and preparation that meant she was ready hours before she needed to be, with much time-checking and curtain twitching until whoever was expected had arrived.

Today was no exception. She had, as always, made an effort with her appearance. Others didn't so much anymore, something which riled her, particularly during the occasional trip to the theatre when she found herself sharing space with people in jeans or trainers.

"It's so disrespectful to the actors" she would say to the same friends who, well used to placating this particular bugbear, would nod compliantly. "And more importantly," she would add, pausing for effect. "It shows a total lack of respect for themselves."

For today's Maltham Historical Society's Golden Jubilee lunch, an event she had been looking forward to, she wore a two-piece grey tweed skirt suit, a Bond Street purchase from the early 80s that had marked a promotion and for that reason she always regarded with a sense of fond nostalgia. It had been unearthed from the rarely used formal section of her wardrobe where garments hung colour coded and draped in polythene in front of rows of nearly identical boxed navy court shoes that she dusted regularly.

The suit was a rather conservative, staid style that had seemed old fashioned at that time, yet in avoiding the sartorial excesses of the period, it had retained a timeless feel and still fitted her well. Her grey/blond hair had been fashioned into a chignon and some light make up had brought some life and colour to a naturally pale complexion and revived her delicate features.

As she looked in the mirror, she was caught by the change in her appearance and how much younger she appeared out of her slacks and fleece jacket. It reminded her of when she was always suited and booted, groomed for work and she was hit by sadness and sense of loss that this part of her life, which had shaped her and consumed her for so long was over for good, a void only heightened by an active mind but lack of hobbies and direction.

The clock told her she had ten minutes to go, and she knew it would be ten minutes because Colin and Miriam were far too conscientious to keep her waiting. She fetched the latest Radio Times and looked out the window over at The Glades, noticing the absent sportscar which meant the husband must have already left for work. The wife's Range Rover was still in position – a bright yellow parking ticket stuck on its windscreen she noted disapprovingly, as the front door opened to release the young boy like a greyhound out of the gate. Dressed in a white tabard with a red cross holding a toy shield he was more animated than usual, jabbing a plastic sword at some imaginary assailant.

The mother, dressed in very little, was on the phone while trying to add a grey felt version of a chainmail helmet to his costume, which once on and fastened, the boy removed and tossed casually onto the driveway. On his feet were lurid, coloured trainers that clashed with the rest of his costume which prompted a rare smile from the older woman who was rarely amused by anything anymore. She watched the woman shout at him to pick up his helmet up.

He ignored her and, as she became more and more absorbed in her call, she ignored him, and the grey bit of cloth remained abandoned in a crumpled ball on the gravel.

The boy looked up at her window and Ms Hobson smiled and waved at him and he waved back before climbing in the back seat of the car.

"Goodbye little man," she said out loud and picked up her handbag as the doorbell rang.

* * *

In many ways the actual gym – as in the room lined with immaculate treadmills and pyramids of gleaming dumbbells was an afterthought to the main activity which centred around the café near reception.

In common with most of the predominantly female membership Carolyn Steadman and her friends owed their physiques more to subtle cosmetic interventions and avoiding pudding than the kind of physical exertion that would compromise their twice weekly blow dries.

Their similar attire and style bore the subtle synergy of an established friendship group, and the eight women ordered coffees and splintered into usual sub camps. It was a demarcation loosely drawn between those who had had some sort of career pre children and the ones who had simply 'married well'. For the former there was an unspoken sense of intellectual superiority, the belief their opinions carried more weight in any meatier discussion, such as they were.

For the latter, the simple one-upmanship derived from knowing they looked better in white jeans or some wispy cocktail dress largely readdressed the balance within a peer group where physical attributes still have a tendency to win out.

Nicky Risling was in the former camp. She had worked as a medical coder in hospitals across the Southeast on a contract basis and still put in the occasional stint if an opportunity arose nearby. It wasn't a vocation or calling, but her efficiency and attention to detail had flourished in a role that demanded both and paid well as she progressed. It also meant she had access to patient medical records which is how she knew that Carolyn hadn't giving birth at London's Queen Victoria hospital, as she claimed, and that being infertile she had not had a baby anywhere.

It was an anomaly, that Nicky had kept to herself, one that would flit in and out of her consciousness depending on life's other distractions or how much the other woman riled her, usually when flirting with her husband.

When she first mentioned that she had worked there to Carolyn, she didn't miss the involuntary twitch of tension in her face. When feeling impish it was a subject she liked to revisit, always intrigued by the fiction that came back when she invented some detail about the maternity ward that Carolyn would purport to remember a little too enthusiastically.

Carolyn's ignorance and naivety, not to have considered that her friend may be privy to this information was no surprise – the woman had never shown any interest in her work or life in general, typical of the self-absorption that had begun to grate on Nicky along with the rest of the group and routine.

She would sit in these coffee mornings watching everyone fall into their usual roles and hierarchies and wonder what had become of her life, a rising sense of desperation fuelled by the knowledge, that this, right now was probably as good as it gets; mortgage paid off, still attractive husband, 2.4 kids, regular holidays. Indeed, life's usual checklist of expectations had been efficiently negotiated and yet she was bored, so bloody bored, particularly with the plastic conversations of the plastic minds around her, as ever devoid of any real point or punchline.

As she sipped her latte and scraped her long red hair into a ponytail, she looked at the others lapping up Carolyn's soliloquy about a baked egg brunch recipe, thinking how could so little consume so much attention. Though what she didn't realise is that rather than actually listening to what the Carolyn woman was saying, most were trying to determine if she had had any work done.

22

Maltham, England, June 2002

Maltham had form when it came to celebrating big events in style and the Queen's Golden Jubilee was no exception. Preparations had consumed the usual troop of volunteers for well over a year, resulting in a packed itinerary and streetscape swathed in red, white, and blue bunting.

In the heavy July air, these flimsy flags barely fluttered. The temperature had risen all week as blue skies transitioned to something muted and cloudier with a sauna like intensity that rendered anyone needing to function dripping and lethargic.

One exception were pupils from Maltham Preparatory School, hyped and impervious to the logistical challenge of being marshalled around a busy town for their jubilee procession.

Relegated to the back of the line due to bad behaviour, Tom Steadman, however, cut a more morose figure, his hot, sticky hand in the fixed grip of junior teacher Laura Lyles who was struggling both with the heat and his tantrums. Sweat dripped steadily down her face and back, flows stymied respectively by the groove under her lower lip and the top of her arse crack as the final headcount took place.

She glanced down at the boy; his curly hair coaxed into stiff side parting; the texture crunchy with gel. His partially unfastened tabard exposed a white vest smeared with grass stains which clung to the small mould of a well-fed stomach, while his face was red with the effort of rage, his loud and attention seeking sobs, immune to any cajoling and appeasement.

An amused colleague said: "Someone's not a happy bunny are they young man" and smiled sympathetically to Laura. Yet it came with the airy detachment of someone free of this particular hassle which only irritated the young woman further as the procession got underway.

* * *

"Ingenious use of product placement!!" quipped the mayor, who in the manner of his predecessors, had acquired an entirely self-appointed quasi-royal status given to spouting lightweight puff and platitudes and waving grandly to members of the public.

Local dignitaries were deliberating over the best dressed window displays, attention currently fixed on the Papier Mache heads of the queen in the opticians, adorned with various brands of sunglasses.

Gavin Smee laughed loud and hard. It was a level of amusement disproportionate to the situation, but he couldn't help himself; it was partly a nerve-fuelled reflex action, but also because he was in his element escorting the party around the high street and elevating his own role to judge and jury rather than the admin bod he was. He was supposed to be writing down the committee's comments, but preferred to focus on his own opinions, a judgement call that had taken on an all-consuming importance.

"Good likeness and attention to detail" - he scribbled with a flourish on his clipboard. He guided the party towards a soft furnishing store taking in the familiar display of armchairs and Afghan rugs that had been doused in gold confetti for the occasion.

He wrote *'more effort needed'* in the appropriate box and assigned a score of 4.5.

"Oh, there you are Ros; Have you checked that the Herald's photographer is on his way; we'll be announcing the winner soon."

The women nodded wearily without enthusiasm. It surprised him, though he didn't comment.

He did not want to encourage a lengthy response or have to listen to any sort of explanation on her well-being, which he guessed was compromised by the heat. He had far more important things to do and people to impress.

Ever conscientious, Ros had of course, phoned the newspaper several times, each time on the receiving end of a different but equally bored and dismissive reporter, wanting her off the line as fast as possible. She was well used to this kind of response but today the negativity bothered her more than usual.

"They said they'd be on their way after they'd finished at the history society lunch," she explained yawning and rubbing her face with a damp tissue. It smudged some of the eyeliner she had forgotten she was wearing, though again Gavin didn't comment.

"Well, that's at the castle, isn't it?" he snapped willing more action and energy from the impassive, doughy face opposite him. "But we have *the mayor* here with us, they really ought to be *here*. Now."

It was naive on his part to expect the press officer to have any sway over the photographer's schedule, but she felt admonished which had been the intention. It was her 24th birthday and she was feeling very down. It was an odd feeling; a detachment only heightened by the revelry all around her; the kind of local community-orientated sense of occasion that was usually her sweet spot and gave her a sense of purpose but today left her feeling sad and numb. She recognised the feeling, most recently from the aftermath of her grandmother's death when she was sad but couldn't cry, unable to get even close to tears, which had then made her feel very guilty.

Now, as it did then, the guilt manifested itself in many odd, random ways, such as when she saw an old person alone on a bench or a dog tied up outside a supermarket. It made her feel inexplicably low, and she would find herself thinking about them many hours later wondering if the dog was abandoned or if the person had spoken to a soul all day and what they were doing now.

Her dissatisfaction was compounded by the hot weather, mainly because of the exhaustion it induced along with heavy sweating and skin chafing. The symptoms were exacerbated by her weight, but for her own convenience, she always preferred to overlook this link, ignoring her GP's advice to take exercise and improve her diet, preferring instead to do her own misguided research and analysis and treating the symptoms as if they were the most unfathomable mystery.

In continually reminding people how debilitating she found the heat, the aim was to pre-empt any loss of efficiency that may be noticed by colleagues though she never felt allowances were made or that people took it seriously. In reality the impact on her performance was negligible anyway.

As always, she had brought her usual hot weather kit which included a handheld fan, a baseball cap, a can of coke, smelling salts, tea tree oil and basic first aid items. Rather than being any use, it simply weighed her down so that every ten minutes or so she would move the bag from shoulder to shoulder to release the tension in her neck and upper back. As she rolled her head from side to side with a pained expression Gavin felt even more irritated; he wanted her to be as upbeat and enthusiastic as him, but he didn't say anything.

* * *

Across town, the 53 members of Maltham historical society milled around the castle as anticipation swelled in advance of their jubilee lunch.

Valerie Hobson had just been dropped off and as a woman who appreciated quality and understatement, she was relieved to see the low rent flags and banners scattered around the rest of the town swopped for tasteful floral garlands. In her opinion, this Jacobean interior needed little adornment.

She had a critical eye, but everywhere she turned, something impressed, especially the elaborate, central table dressed in heavy white linen cloth and solid silverware. She inspected the name plate holders that took the form of miniature crowns, along with the individual menus written out on parchment scrolls, smiling and making small, appreciative noises to herself at the attention to detail.

As the society chairman and vice president nodded in her direction, she raised her glass of sherry, in part greeting, part show of appreciation before circling the table to find her seat. Most names were written in silver, gold, or bronze to denote the individual's membership status, but struggling to read the silver font she put on her glasses before taking another lap of table.

"Oh, Val you're not on this one, you're seated right over there love; through there."

Bristling, Valerie took off her glasses and looked around her to see the vice chairman's girlfriend Pauline Mansfield gesturing towards an annexed room in the distance. She ignored her until the woman came over and gently but firmly took her elbow steering her past familiar faces and the Herald photographer who was already getting a line up shot of the small group who had deliberately hovered nearby in the hope of being snapped.

The two women arrived at a small, empty box room which despite some effort had not escaped the feel of what it was - a ten-year-old conservatory – entirely devoid of the main building's 17th century majesty. A small circular table laid for seven people, bore all the hallmarks of an overspill while her name plate (written in biro) had rechristened her Vanessa.

"Oh, first one here - nice and cosy, isn't it?" chivvied Paula as if consigning a reluctant elderly relative to a nursing home.

"For God's sake this won't do," Valerie muttered, her heart rate quickening with indignation.

She looked at Paula with her painted-on smile who either hadn't heard or pretended not to, taking in her low-cut blouse and crepy cleavage, face encased in matte foundation which clung to dry skin and large open pores. Every feature was over-drawn – lipliner that extended well beyond the natural mouth line, eyes rimmed with thick black pencil that had smudged in the heat. It was the pick-thin high heels though which prompted an involuntary tut.

Stiletto shoes had long been banned in the great hall to preserve the delicate marble flooring, and she thought how typical it was of someone like her not to know that key detail.

Brazen enough to be either oblivious or untroubled by other people's judgements and feelings Paula continued: "Now because you and a few others are on your own and we had an odd number we thought it would be easier to put you in here. I think you will find it a lovely little group Val, lots of lively chit chat guaranteed."

She patted the chair as if gesturing to a dog to sit down which Valerie found herself doing, wincing at the phrase chit chat, being patronised and treated like a doddery fool by a woman all of five years her junior who used to work in the town's discount shoe shop.

She recalled the one time she went in that shoe shop searching for navy courts and overheard Paula asking her manager what penultimate meant.

"Oh, yes, one other thing, we've had a cancellation from the person who would have been on your left," Paula added filling the silence and gesturing to the empty chair, "Nice bit of extra space – you can get your elbows out and spread out properly. I'll leave you to enjoy."

She had been talking to Valerie's back, which remained unturned, her eyes fixed ahead on a small sign that reminded the castle staff to stack the chairs and put to one side when the room was not in use and to not smoke on the premises.

The tap of Paula's heels signalled her retreat to the main hall as Valerie now looked up at the ceiling blankly, breathing heavily while debating whether to walk out.

The words repeated on a loop in her head as her face burned with indignation.

'*We thought we'd put you here....*' Who the hell did she think she was talking to and what possible interest did that old tart have in local history? The woman had only joined the society three months ago because she was sleeping with the vice chairman, now she was lording it around, playing hostess and dictating where she, a long-term gold status member, sat at a major event. What in god's name could she contribute to any discussion with a historical bent? She doesn't even know what penultimate means. And since when did being single preclude you from sitting in the main room? This seemed to be the very worst discrimination.

A man who seemed very young to her but was probably in his mid-30s took his seat opposite and after a brief acknowledgement turned his attention to the menu. Valerie recognised him but couldn't place him before realising that he worked at the castle and usually managed the catering teams at the venue.

The rest of the table arrived soon afterwards, including the castle's press officer and someone thinking of joining the society who had been allowed to attend the dinner for free, all in all a line up dismissed in her mind as deeply disappointing and beneath her as she sighed deeply and tried to keep calm.

As a waiter appeared with a bottle of Sauvignon her bony hand covered the top of her wine glass on auto pilot, teal-coloured veins stark and raised across thin, pale flesh.

"Do you have elderflower cordial"?

"Sorry madam, I don't understand," he said in a foreign accent which was just another irritation.

"Well would you like to find someone who does."

"Sorry madam you would like me to do *what*"?

"CAN YOU PLEASE FIND SOMEONE WHO CAN GET ME A GLASS OF ELDERFLOWER CORDIAL."

The aim was to be heard above the buzz from the main room, but the tone and volume stood out for its stridence and surprised the rest of the table now studying her properly for the first time with mild curiosity.

"Oh, never mind, don't bother." She waved her hand in his direction as if swotting away a fly without looking before reaching for the water jug. Too many ice cubes fell into her glass as she poured, along with a few wilted mint leaves and cucumber.

"Since when did a drink of water come with a salad," she said to no one in particular, prompting a couple of tepid smiles from the others before they returned to the menu.

She pulled at the collar of her tweed jacket that now felt hot and itchy in a room that lacked the cool air of the main hall, the glass roof trapping the rising heat like a greenhouse.

The animated conversations in the next room only amplified the stilted silence in the annexe with this small group struggling to match the enthusiasm. The situation needed someone to take the lead and create their own sub party, but no one could be bothered.

Primed as ever to any perceived slight, Valerie noticed one or two on the table already straining to see the action elsewhere and rolled her eyes. She thought it was an appalling lack of respect and effort not to focus their attention on where they were and who they were with. It was this consistent failure of others to toe the line and meet her expectations compounded by her own lack of self-awareness that made her life so exasperating.

She took another sip of water, a tiny mint leaf adhering to her lipstick which she whipped off angrily. From what she could glean, the talk next door seemed more general gossip than anything to do with local history. God how things had changed, she thought. She took a bread roll offered from a small basket and looked down at the notes peaking from handbag.

It was research she had enjoyed doing over the past few days on the town's previous royal celebrations that she was going to refer to but was now superfluous with the present company unworthy of her musings. She had expected good conversation with likeminded people, who if perhaps not quite her intellect equal, would come close but sadly it wasn't to be.

* * *

The school procession stuttered past the usual landmarks including the crying boy war memorial and the blue plaques of notable residents, all highlighted earnestly by staff to their distracted charges who weren't listening. Tom Steadman's sword scraped along the pavement with grating repetition, though he remained undeterred by the threats of confiscation much to his teacher's frustration.

Laura had never warmed to him, finding him childish, even for a four a year-old boy, a limited vocabulary, a tendency for noise, gestures, and fuss rather than the more sophisticated linguistic development of his peers. Plus, she didn't like the way his mind worked; how when a car appeared, he would pull at her arm as if about to run in front of it or keep coming to a standstill like a poorly trained dog, that needed more manhandling.

Predictably her head had started to throb, and a dizziness crept in whenever she moved it quickly from one side to another, it was the usual preamble to full blown migraine, the kind that would distort her vison and make her feel nauseous and in need of a lie down and because of the inevitability of this outcome, she was feeling more and more miserable.

For the last ten minutes or so she had fantasised about her preferred choice of activity on a day like this; watching Wimbledon or sat in the garden in shorts, bare feet cushioned on the lawn with a glass of something cold, but there was still so much of this day to endure.

She watched her colleagues in the distance, bossy and boring as ever, seizing every opportunity for some sort of lecture or learning with their young charges. She had assumed primary school teaching especially at a home counties prep may have been her calling, or perhaps, more accurately, an easy life: but the reality was proving very different.

Unlike most of the staff here she hadn't been through the independent school system herself, and as her paranoia and dissatisfaction grew, she wondered if this discrepancy had a bearing on the kind dogsbody jobs frequently assigned to her, like today's particular duty with the problem child.

Or perhaps it was her disinclination to adopt the quasi-parental role that many of the staff did with the pupils that marked her out. She could, in fact, take or leave whether the boys reached their full potential or many of the other lofty expectations Heralded in the school prospectus, an ambivalence that sometimes took effort to disguise.

To her, most of them were indulged little arseholes, utterly ungrateful for the privileged cards they had been dealt and the life of a comfort and connections lay ahead regardless of their mediocre abilities, none more so than Tom Steadman.

The procession snaked around the edge of the supermarket carpark and the art college towards the high street, from which loud music and the general buzz of noise and activity stirred the restless energy of the boys. Barriers erected that morning in anticipation of crowds had seemed optimistic but as people gathered three deep on the pavement the occasion was starting to live up to its billing.

In no mood to make small talk with her colleagues, Laura was happy to hang back a little from the rest of the line as she watched Tom toss the sword casually into the road.

"It can bloody well stay there, you little shit," she found herself saying out loud.

He looked up at her quizzically as if seeing her for the first time.

"What?"

"Never you mind. You're not getting it back. That's it."

Not that he really cared about the sword anymore.

"You said shit," he shouted it at the top of his voice as the other boys nearby turned around always receptive to some fresh, rebellious diversion and started laughing.

"No, I didn't," snapped Laura. "Stop making up stories."

"You said shit, you said shit, you said shit, you said shit."

And now the little flashes of light and inability to focus began, a pixelated, distorted vision that signalled her migraine had arrived and would last for approximately the next ten minutes.

She let go of the boy's hand, dried her damp palm along the side of her trousers and sifted through the junk in her rucksack to retrieve her water bottle, her dry throat gulping much of its contents in one hit.

Frantic fingers felt for a few almond nuts that she knew were still in the lining or pocket.

The sense of relief of finally finding one almost made her smile as if it was some elixir that could eradicate a headache that several paracetamols wouldn't shift.

More water gulped fast to the last drop and the moisture in the mouth was instantly soothing as she took several deep breaths, eyes closed briefly for some relief from the distortion and flashing lights.

When they opened, she only saw the worried, startled face of the deputy head teacher.

It was just inches away and as she looked up, she realised that everyone was staring at her.

"Laura! Where is Tom Steadman?"

23

Maltham, England, June 2002

The boy standing in front of her was an intriguing proposition. Dressed in a depleted version of a costume that no doubt looked different when he left the house that morning, his face was red and blotchy, the residue of tears and tantrum. Now, with the worst of it subsided, he seemed subdued, lost and receptive to a sympathetic adult ready to take charge.

Ros knelt down looking at his large brown eyes and thick lashes, full, rounded cheeks and felt protective, the first feeling that day other than numbness and negativity. She had a maternal instinct but even with her youth she was resigned to this only ever being channelled through her adored cats or her relative's offspring, she would see occasionally. When it came to the opposite sex, she was as naive and chaste as the heroines in the trashy period romance, she consumed avidly existing in a world of crushes and fantasy with little interest in reality and the physical mechanics.

"Are you lost sweetie?"

He nodded shyly, looking up at the large figure looming over him.

"Were you with your mummy?"

An exaggerated shake of the head.

"My teacher," he offered finally "She sweared at me; she called me a shit."

"Did she? Well, she's very naughty then, isn't she?"

The boy nodded hard.

The press officer took his hand relishing its feel, which was warm, small and soft, running her thumb back and forth against the smoothest skin yet to be dried, burnt or unsullied life's wear and tear.

"What's your name?"

"Tom"

"Well, I have an idea, Tom; why don't we have a little walk around together until we find your friends and teachers, how does that sound, eh?

"What's your name?" he asked confidently

She paused briefly, unused to lying.

"Mary. You can call me Mary."

The boy nodded, comfortable with his new companion, happy for her to take the lead. The pair walked along the main high street past the crowds whose collective attention fell on

the floats and their waving occupants riding past as loud music blasted from the speakers.

As she steered him along the busy pavement the young woman was enjoying this very rare feeling of control and the sense of purpose she always craved, though what exactly that was, in this moment, was unclear as she guided him away from the rest of humanity towards the fag end of town, where the discount shoe store and a Wimpy bar were the most tempting outlets. The listless exhaustion that had swamped her earlier had temporarily lifted. She felt useful, energised and alive.

* * *

A tinkle of a spoon on the wine glass signalled the start of the after-dinner speeches. Valerie Hobson stayed where she was. The rest of her table had left their seats and wandered into the main hall to listen to the speakers, but she refused to join them. Standing in a line at the back like street urchins looking through a window of a shop they weren't allowed in was one indignity too far.

Instead, she stared ahead at the sign reminding staff where to put the chairs and not to smoke indoors, her modest mouth set in an angry little line as she breathed heavily.

All the jokes and platitudes from the speeches next door faded into a background drone. Under normal circumstances and in a better mood it was the sort of fodder that would prompt a polite smile from her, even a small chuckle to show willing and that she did have a sense of humour in spite of the slightly abrasive exterior. Now, it was just the repeated roll of her eyes. The only other person still at the table was the youngish castle employee who had returned his attention to the menu to avoid eye contact and small talk.

Not that she minded. She was busy mentally drafting the various complaint letters and toying with further action she might take. Should she resign from the society? Propose a vote of no confidence in the chair? Would anyone care? She used to think her opinion counted for something but after today she had never felt more inconsequential.

Perhaps she could illicit opinion from a few other senior members who she respected but the reality was that they were in the other room enjoying themselves and for that reason equally culpable as everyone else; the depressing reality was that she was too angry with too many people to know who to target first. Whatever the option, there would be consequences she thought as she took quick, little successive sips of water and dabbed a bead of sweat on her chin with her napkin.

She looked at her plate and the mush of several uneaten strawberries in a melted pool of bright pink sorbet and the dollop of meringue minus one, small bite. It was unusual for her to leave food, because even with her modest appetite she hated any kind of waste. It was why in the run up to an event like this, she always avoided breakfast and ate very lightly the night before as she had done yesterday.

Unfortunately, circumstances had ensured she didn't feel hungry at all and that every admittedly delicious mouthful from the duck pate, coronation chicken and strawberry sorbet served with buttery crown-shaped shortbread had become an endurance, she may as well have been eating a packet of stale crisps.

Another burst of raucous laughter. This one was gathering steam, segueing into a prolonged and spirited applause over some punchline she couldn't hear. Some people were banging their hands on the table in hysterics as if playing bongos.

"What did they say?" she snapped crossly to the man opposite rereading the starter choices

"Couldn't catch it I'm afraid."

"Well, you wouldn't because you're stuck in here in this bloody room. Oh, for God's sake this won't do."

He looked at her with a puzzled expression as he sipped his wine.

Curiosity finally getting the better of her, she shot up from her seat to see what she was missing, irritated to see those who had moved in there from her table bothering to applaud something they had never really part of. For the first time she looked properly at the main room, her tired eyes scanning the familiar faces, many wiping tears of laughter from faces reddened with alcohol and good food, tables heaving with bottles and glasses – a party she had never really been at.

Some were laughing so much, they looked as if they might collapse or combust, most the wrong side of 60 and not in the best shape, struggling with the temperature and excess food and drink were loosening ties and undoing a couple of buttons for comfort.

Her eyes now fell on Paula, horrified how close she was sitting to the chairman, almost on his lap with no restraint or respect for the occasion or surroundings. Every time the woman lent in to speak to him, her top gaped open to expose more sun damaged décolletage, which was probably the intention, thought Valerie with a shake of the head.

By the time the waiters reappeared with coffee canisters on trolleys, she had had enough and scooped up her handbag from under her chair and swiped away the crease her skirt.

Pushing down hard on the silver bar on the emergency exit door, partly in temper, the woman was released into the grounds, the distant shouts from one of waiting staff cutting out as it slammed shut behind her.

She was in a part of the grounds she had never seen before. The grass was parched, brown and scrubbier than the pristine walled gardens round the front, a neglect she found disappointing and lazy, like a dress being held in place by safety pins at the back. It was also difficult to walk on in her heeled court shoes, which she was less used to wearing these days, yet fired up with indignation she had a wired energy and made steady progress as she began the long, hot walk home.

* * *

The noise and crowds of the town were long forgotten as Ros and Tom continued their rhythmic plod to nowhere. They had walked around two miles, the four-year-old keeping up with the woman's pace, uncomplaining and not especially curious over their whereabouts. He wore her baseball cap, which she had told him was to shield him from the sun, but it wasn't sunny and for reasons she did not fully know or understand herself, it was really so that he would be inconspicuous. It was also why the last remnants of his costume had been removed and put in her rucksack which left him in just a vest, shorts, long white socks and black pumps as if he was about to do a PE lesson.

By now the clammy flesh around her groin and armpits was starting to irritate and as someone who never drank water unless it was an emergency her mouth was very dry. She was uncomfortable but didn't want to stop, reluctant to disrupt their progress as they passed pockets of anonymous grey blocks of office where lanyard-wearing workers puffed on fags in the doorway, part of the depleted, skeleton teams working on this public holiday. Unburdened from this grey, watch-checking conformity Ros felt a rare rush of excitement, though it was tempered by the anxiety and the knowledge that she was not really free at all and at some point, there would have to be explanations and excuses.

On their right was the Chinese restaurant that always looked closed while the leisure centre came up on their left, its clock reading 3pm – late enough now for the woman to start considering how she would explain her absence to her employers, though she suspected she wouldn't be missed.

Her only real duty that day was to a stay in the town centre and make notes on the various Jubilee activities and celebrations. From this she would write up a press release and send it to the usual handful of contacts including the Maltham Herald and local radio who would delete her email as soon as her name appeared in the address without reading it.

Afterwards she would start the time-consuming round up of

follow up calls to see if the release was of interest, before logging their response – usually 'no' or 'unavailable' in a spreadsheet – a different font for each media outlet - all of which in that moment she could see with the starkest clarity was as pointless as everyone else did.

She looked down at the small figure slowing a little in pace. She reasoned her disappearance would be far less obvious than during a more typical day in the office – but it still couldn't go unnoticed. As a dullard who lived to follow other people's rules, she was unused to having or needing the kind of initiative to invent plausible excuses for any rogue activity that deviated from the usual routine. It was all overwhelming her to such an extent that she decided to abandon this chain of thought for the time being and focus on the enjoying the here and now.

Ahead of her she could see the bus bound for the next town waiting at the stop, its signal flashing as the driver, ahead of schedule, passed some time reading a newspaper. Options and consequences flitted around her head; she wouldn't run, as she didn't run for anything, or even quicken the pace but, with no other ideas forthcoming, this would make the decision for her. If it was still there when they caught up, they would get on, if it drove off, they would turn back. She began to fumble in her bag for her purse, finding a couple of pound coins.

"Are we getting on the bus Mary," Tom asked.

"Yes, I think we are."

"I never go on buses. Where are we going?"

"On an adventure – do you like adventures Tom?"

He nodded and ran ahead a little.

* * *

The long, hot walk was calming Val Hobson's mind. As was her way, she had used the time wisely, mentally composing complaint letters to the historical society over her treatment and the general decline in its standards, a rant that was shaping up nicely and she was eager to get down on paper.

Her route avoided the main hub of the centre and the crowds, though music and laughter were never that far away. People she passed were in high spirits that against the odds slightly lifted her own and she exchanged brief smiles with various family groups wishing that more days were like this – people being friendly, community-spirited, less preoccupied with themselves and in their own worlds.

The flipside was the amount of rubbish generated. Her eyes scanned the pavement disapprovingly taking in the strands of bunting that had come loose, the discarded paper cups and plates spewing out of over-stuffed bins which was when she noticed an unfamiliar coin.

Groaning slightly as she crouched awkwardly, she inspected the 20 Franc piece, one she hadn't seen in some time and put it in her handbag.

* * *

Carolyn Steadman's hand was trembling too hard to dial the number, so she abandoned the plan throwing it across the kitchen just missing the coffee machine. Sat at the breakfast bar, on the high and hard steel stool her entire body was shaking, and she felt an odd disorientation, as if she was losing connection with reality and her physical surroundings and could faint.

She dragged herself up grabbing any surface she could to get to the kitchen door which she opened and stepped outside. Her relief at the faintest breeze across her face was short-lived as a wave of nausea stirred, and she threw up on the marble slabs of patio. This familiar act seemed to purge the most acute of her emotions as she began to feel the solidity of the step underneath and the cool marble under her bare feet. Eventually she got up and retrieved her phone, dialling her husband's number again as she went into the front room and watched police calling at the house opposite.

"David, it's Carolyn. The police have just been here."

"The police? Shit, what's happened?"

"They've, they've ...."

She felt breathless again, the effort and enormity of trying to form any coherent sentence, temporarily beyond her physical and mental strength.

"Right, Carolyn, calm down, whatever it is just tell me."

"They said that Tom has gone missing from his school jubilee procession...

"Missing? When?"

"This afternoon, around 2pm, well that's when they noticed he wasn't there."

"2 pm? It's, it's gone 4 now, what the hell are they playing at, why have we only just been

told?"

"They've been trying to get hold of both of us all afternoon – I've been at the gym, then lunch at Sorrentino with my phone off. They were sat on the drive when I got here... and where were you? They tried your mobile and the school tried it and your office with no answer for hours..."

"I've been with a client."

"But that's not it, that's not all," continued Carolyn.

"What?"

"When I saw them, the police car, you know what I thought? I thought that was it, that they'd found us out and it was all over and when they told me what it was, what had happened, I felt, I felt...."

"You felt what?"

"Relief, some kind of relief.... can you believe that, can you actually believe that? What sort of person does that make me... what sort of mother does that make me? Relief that their son's gone missing for the second time and they're not going to get in trouble over the first time."

She was laughing now, an odd high-pitched shriek that she couldn't stop. Her rational side knew it was anything but funny, yet in the moment, the absurdity of the scenario had become darkly hysterical.

"Caz, look you need to calm yourself down and keep it together. Look I'll be there as soon as I can. What have the police said? Shit is there anyone there hearing this?"

"Don't be stupid, of course not. The police told me to wait here, in case he arrives back.

"David, I can't believe this is happening. How the hell can this be happening?"

"Look do as they say, stay put and I'll be back soon."

"Well, how long?"

"I dunno, an hour maybe, depending on traffic, I'll come straightway.

"An hour? Where the hell are you"

"As I said, with client, look I'll be as quick as I can. Love you."

The man pressed the phone under his chin as if trying to penetrate the jawbone, eyes shut as he processed the most cataclysmic interruption to his afternoon.

"David are you alright, what's happened?" asked his young colleague in the hotel bed.

"It's my son, Tom, he's gone missing."

"Missing? Oh my god – from where?"

"Sorry, I don't have time to talk."

He put on his trousers and churned through the various cushions and throws that had fallen across the bedroom floor until he found his shirt and car keys.

"Look I've got to go, I'll call."

He shut the door and was in his car in seconds.

* * *

The speed with which the bus sailed past familiar streetscapes to more uncertain territory unnerved the woman for the first time.

It reminded her of the times when she couldn't face school and instead of getting off at the right bus stop with the rest of the kids, she would stay on, shrinking into the back seat on the top deck wishing she could just stay there for ever and not have face anyone. It was similar feeling to back then in the sense that a significant decision had been made, a line crossed with the inevitable repercussions and the enormity of what she was doing now clear, all earlier anticipation, choice and plausible explanations had transitioned to worry and consequences.

She looked at the boy's legs swinging faster against the seat head turning from side to side as he absorbed his new surroundings, rubbing a sweaty nose and wiping the damp hand on his vest. He was getting more restless and looking at her a little more critically like the stranger she was, small hands set in tight fists with growing unease.

"We're on our way, soon be there just going different route," she said, aiming for soothing reassurance to ward off the first stirring of discontent.

"And if you're a good boy perhaps we can get an ice cream when we arrive, would you like that?"

He didn't answer his previously neutral face now set in a sulkier expression, eyes in a determined glare, a hint of rebellion brewing.

She found the last tissue from her packet and wiped her sweaty face, surprised to see black smears of makeup that she forgotten she was wearing. She screwed up the damp ball and tossed it under their seat, before looking around guiltily in case anyone noticed, seeing only a couple of teenagers preoccupied with something that had kept them in hysterics on and off for the past 10 minutes.

They would get off at the next stop she decided, she couldn't risk a tantrum that would draw attention, though being as anonymous as she was meant it was unlikely anyway. In contrast to many young girls her age, she never got a first glance let along a second one.

The bus began to slow down as it approached a small wooden shelter on the dual carriage way. It was one of those stops that looked like it would be purgatory to have to wait at; set on the edge of a busy bypass, a pile of smashed glass on the pavement in front of a vandalised window and doused in obscene graffiti.

Through the window she took in the crude phallic illustrations that had prompted more hysteria from the back of the bus. She was shocked and embarrassed by the level of detail, some spiky hairs daubed onto a pair of giant testicles she noticed as well as disgusting language. She thought of the many old people that relied on local buses who would have to wait at this stop and see all of this, stark and graphic in broad daylight.

Would they mutter their disapproval to another passenger or pretend not to notice while talking about the weather? And now that odd flat, guilty feeling was stirring in her again, as thoughts of their awkwardness which transitioned into a broader feeling of unease and tension throughout her body.

She pressed the bell and took Tom's hand as they walked unsteadily down the aisle, him trying to press the rest of the bells they passed, her hand decisively moving his away each time to stop him.

"Thank you, driver," she said eyes fixed on the door, willing it to open quicker.

"If you want Selby then you better stay on for the next stop love. We can get you a bit nearer than this."

"No, it's fine, we'll walk, we could do with some fresh air."

"Are you sure, it's quite a trek"

"Yep, no problem, thanks"

The doors that were smeared with a day or maybe weeks' worth of sweaty handprints opened with a loud hiss, leaving the fumy waft from the engine as a parting shot as the pair stood on the pavement, looking equally lost and disorientated. It was uncharacteristically quiet, as the odd lorry thundered past, and the woman tried to swot away the flies drawn to an overflowing bin as she tried to get her bearings.

"I'm tired Mary. Don't want to walk. I'm hungry, I want a biscuit," said the boy while stabbing the end of his trainers on the dusty pavement defiantly.

"Well, we can't stay here by this busy road can we," she chivvied trying hard to appear calm and in control. "Now, come on you'll spoil your shoes they're getting scuffed and dirty, aren't they?"

She took his hand again, summoning up some effort to keep her voice and demeanour bright but assertive which appeared to work with him and while he remained sullen, he cooperated and as they headed in the direction of Selby. The pace had slowed now as both were tired and in need of a break and food, shoes rubbing on moist feet, mouths dry, and no water left.

"Right, very soon we'll be there, and we can sit down and have a nice cold drink and something sweet, can't we, doesn't that sound lovely?"

She was trying to convince herself as much as him.

"Then am I going home?" he asked.

"Well, that's where we're going," she lied looking up at a slate sky on the cusp of a storm.

"Not much longer now."

* * *

Her feet were moist from sweat and a burst blister seeping through her tights. It was just another discomfort for Valerie Hobson to bear during this final stretch of the journey along with the scorching heat and parched throat as she swept past the familiar pristine hedges that edged the houses in The Glades.

Shaped into hard, angular blocks, they bordered the sleek landscaped but flower-lite front lawns that made her think as she always did, that for all the scope and value of these properties, their modern uniformity rendered them lacklustre and classless. Head down, eyes set in a squint, a dogged determination had made light work of the three-mile march from the castle in the afternoon peak heat with only the sight of the police car in the Steadman's drive stopping her fevered pace.

This sudden inertia unleashed a wave of pain through her feet and legs and made her wince as she removed a foot from her shoe and glanced cautiously at the damage before staring again at the property though there was little to derive from the exterior.

If there had been an accident it was unlikely to involve the wife with her 4x4 on the drive, she deduced. She took out the other foot and rotated the ankle, her eyes darting to the presence of police officers at the end of her own road, doing door to door enquiries. She hurried towards her own property whipping past the familiar tangle of roses and pear trees that lined the path to her front door keen to be there when they called.

Like a darts player on the cusp of a throw she held the key in front of her as an entirely new thought entered her head. It had pierced the repetitious loop replaying the afternoon's indignities and frustrations and was ominous enough to send a chill through her hot body. As the door unlocked, she wondered if what she had seen earlier was connected and if indeed, it had been the boy who lived opposite.

* * *

Tom began to run as soon as he saw the small café. It sat between a post office and Co-op, which were both closed and represented the sum total of amenities in what constituted the main drag in this pin prick of place whose population had migrated to Maltham for the Jubilee celebrations.

Fearing it was shut along with everything else, the woman was extremely relieved to see the boy open the door and go inside. She followed shortly afterwards, greeting the girl serving, who looked about 16 and like she didn't want to be there. She eventually handed them menus.

The pair sat outside, surveying the cake and milkshake options each one illustrated with a bright, garish photo which had further piqued the boy's enthusiasm and transformed his demeanour, now he was fully distracted by this all-important task.

Usually denied such sugary excess at home, he chose a chocolate milkshake with extra whipped cream and chocolate fudge cake. Ros plumped for the same and when their order arrived, they both tucked in, sitting in comfortable silence bar the odd approving noise, a simple harmony as both spoons scraped the bottom of their glasses to collect every last molten drop.

For Ros, it had been a brief and well needed reprieve from the pressure of boosting the boy's mood and keeping him compliant but now they'd finished, it wouldn't last, none of this could and by now it was already over. She took the cue when he went to the toilet.

"You can manage, can't you? Go back inside and ask the lady on the counter where they are."

He nodded to where she pointed, his small frame soon disappearing from sight once the door was closed.

She stared ahead at the corn fields – a vast expanse of mustard yellow that swayed and rippled in the wind that was stirring. Against this blank canvas with no distractions, her thoughts became bullets pounding around her head, competing for supremacy,

The guiltiness, her colleague's insults, Gavin Smee being cross, the Herald being rude, old people alone on benches and being exposed to rude graffiti at bus stops, guilt, worry, dread and now a deep longing to be home in familiar surroundings, free of this entirely self-induced pressure and responsibility that had given her an awful headache.

Ros looked behind through the café window at the girl reading a magazine, smirking at something on the page. She turned back to the joyless beauty in front of her, then grabbed her bag and ran to the bus stop, perhaps the first time she had run in a year, the rarest burst of exertion that left her crimson-faced and panting.

She didn't have long to wait and when the bus arrived bound to Maltham she stumbled up the steps to the top deck, steadying herself by grabbing the series of headrests she passed before falling into the back seat, heart racing and sweat dripping.

She closed her eyes and tried to steady her breathing which was hard and fast inducing a wave of panic that she hadn't experienced for some time.

One, elephant, two elephant, three elephant, four elephant, five elephant.... she counted in her head, until the breathing slowed down.

Like abandoning a baby on a hospital step, she reasoned she had done the responsible thing; that Tom would be fine where he was. The girl in the café would take charge, phone the police or perhaps take him to the station herself; all would be sorted; he wasn't the kind of child that people would ignore; they would be concerned and protective as she had been; he would soon be looked after and returned to his parents.

It was a clumsy and implausibly neat summation that still brought some comfort as she watched the first spots of rain fall on the window. She undid her shoes, releasing her fat, swollen and throbbing feet and closed her eyes listening to the rain tapping softly; she had always liked that sound, finding it comforting and cosy and as the bus headed closer to home, she felt calmer and relieved to be returning to some normality now too exhausted and without the capacity to worry about any deeper consequences.

Tom Steadman came out of the café restroom and passed the counter unnoticed by the girl who had her back to him and was on the phone. He opened the door to find Ros gone. He stared hard and puzzled at the two empty glasses and plates left on the table. After a brief look at the deserted street, he headed in the direction of the fields and towards a wooded outcrop, feeling an unexpected chill for the first time that day as the rain began to soak his clothes.

Ten minutes later the waitress cleared the two empty glasses and picked up the £10 payment.

24

England, 2002

Ros Cowley's key stabbed a little at the front door of her parent's cottage as an unseen helicopter whirred overhead in the distance. Shutting the door on its drone and the drama she extricated her swollen feet from her shoes and absorbed the comforting familiarity of the hallway.

The scene was as she left it this morning which seemed so very long ago now it could have been last week. Her mother's National Trust shopping bag hung on the end of the banister, three bags of clothes earmarked for the Oxfam shop and a pile of read library books to be returned were lined up by the door.

On the small table, by the phone were three theatre tickets to see an Alan Ayckbourn play that weekend.

She left her bag near the stairs and walked into the spotless kitchen, her bare, sore feet relishing the soft carpet and then the cool smack from the lino as she filled the teapot watching her father through the window, building a small bonfire, it's sweet, woody scent wafting through the house.

The girl took in his calm, focus as he deliberated over which bit of kindling to add next, a decision which at the moment was really or he had to worry about. It stirred emotion in her over what she may have inflicted on this quiet, inoffensive little man carefully building his bonfire who had spent his life doing the right thing, as she had until today. How oblivious he was to a drama he risked being part of by proxy.

Only now did she remember her thirst, odd given her arid throat. She gulped down a glass of water reminding herself she couldn't become emotional which would make her vulnerable and run the risk of losing control.

Before the tears came, she shouted out the window to ask if he wanted a tea which made him jump and his eyes dart around to detect the direction of the voice.

"Yes, please," he gave her a quick wave. "Glad you've got back ok; your mother rang after her Zumba class - said a load of local roads were closed off due some police business. Did you hear of anything? She says she she'll pick up fish and chips when she can."

"No, nothing. I could always cook something."

"Well, you could, but don't go to too much trouble if you've been working all day – how did the jubilee celebrations go? I was going to nip into town myself but got distracted with all the gardening that needing doing."

"Yes, good, very busy. There's some of that salami and the goats cheese left – could do us all a salad."

"Apparently, the crowds were three or four deep according to next door," he said.

He was taking off his gardening gloves and inspecting something on the palm of his hand as he walked into the kitchen.

"Ros, did you take the first aid stuff with you this morning?"

"Yep – in my bag, by the stairs. Actually, I think I'll make some rock cakes. Right, what do I need, what do I need?"

She began walking around the kitchen, opening random drawers and cupboards with no thought or idea as to what she was looking for while her mind raced - buses, milkshakes, Gavin Smee being disappointed, the abandoned boy and where he would be now.

It was as if the more she could drown in the normal and pedestrian, the more alien and abstract the past few hours would seem, almost as if they'd never happened.

She lifted the lid off the china hen that sat by the breadbin which emitted its usual loud clucking noise as she grabbed four eggs and studied their smooth, identical form.

"Have you found it Dad?"

"Not yet. My God, what have you got in here, I've never seen so much stuff?"

She could hear the faint sound of items churning, zipping and unzipping and his soft groan as he sat down on the stairs.

"Hats, fans and some giant St George flag by the looks of things," he continued in the distance. "Surprised you haven't done your back in lugging this around. Right here is, just need a plaster."

A chill shot through her as she opened the cupboard, trembling hand trying to locate the cinnamon in a tub packed with other spices in identikit little pots. Turmeric, ginger, cardamon. Each one was pulled out and slammed back in place as her breathing quickened and she abandoned the task. Under a greying sky, the unguarded fire was losing some momentum without its earlier careful tending.

The young woman took a deep breath as she impatiently brushed the sweat from her face and forced out a bright, casual tone as her father came into the kitchen.

"Why don't you sit down for a bit in the front room have your tea, you look tired.".

"Ok. I might just do that."

She shut the front room door behind him quickly before grabbing her bag from the hall and removing Tom Steadman's tabard, scrunching it in her hand like a dishcloth. Hurrying into the garden, she followed the small path that led to the shed, greenhouse and a fire which she stoked with a bit of branch. She tossed the flimsy garment on top, prodding it deeper into the belly of the flames and watched the cheap nylon evaporate in seconds.

* * *

A pair of scuffed navy court shoes, bearing the effects of her long walk home sat on a sheet of newspaper by her armchair, a small tin of shoe polish and brush by the side.

Having given her statement and shown the police out, a familiar listlessness was already stirring in the silence of Valerie Hobson's living room, the come down after a day of intense stimulus, heightened by this fresh, unfolding drama.

The woman was no clearer in her own mind over the significance of what she had seen earlier on her walk home. However, she felt she had been listened to and taken seriously which in view of the day's earlier events at the castle had seemed a small bonus. She told the officers how around forty minutes into her walk home from the castle she had taken a shortcut which brought her out to Broadwalk Hill near a bus stop and bent down to pick up a coin on the pavement, peering at what was French currency.

Still crouched, she looked up and directly in her line of vision, she saw a child's feet being lifted from the pavement onto a bus. She had thought quite absently that the shoes – trainers with bright lime and maroon colouring were familiar and realised that was because they were similar to or identical to a pair worn by the boy who lives opposite whom she now knows as Tom Steadman and who was wearing them when he left for school that morning.

Asked why she had noticed and remembered this detail she replied that the incongruity of the footwear worn with his St George's knight costume had stood out and made her smile. She had waved at him, and he waved back which pleased her, because while she wasn't really a 'children sort of person' she felt a fondness towards him.

Even though she didn't know him, she could tell he was 'a little character, strong willed and seemed to know his own mind'. No, she couldn't be sure at all that the boy getting on the bus was the same child or if they were being coerced as almost all of his body was obscured by other people who she couldn't remember other than a youngish ginger-haired man nor did notice where the bus was bound for.

Perhaps ordinarily she would have, but she had been in a flustered state after a very difficult afternoon and was hot and tired and keen to get back to her house. It was only when she saw the police car in the Steadman's drive that it occurred to her there could be a connection.

The police wrote all of this down and thanked her leaving their card in case anything else came to mind. She pulled the curtain back to see their car pulling away before looking at the house opposite, with its drawn curtains and busy drive and thought of the boy and his stocky frame and wondered if he still had his sword with him which he had seem so attached to.

Ordinarily, the uncertainty of such a drama and one she may even have a small part to play in would consume her, yet she still felt so flat and so very disappointed.

She briefly considered calling round to the Steadmans to tell them what she had told the police. It would have been a justifiable opportunity to introduce herself she reasoned, yet she was hit by both a crushing fatigue and the depressing realisation that they were unlikely to recognise her in spite of the fact she lived opposite and felt like she knew them.

Even in view of the difficult circumstances, she knew this would irritate and be further confirmation of her growing invisibility and irrelevance and after a day full of slights and disrespect and she couldn't face anymore.

Out of habit she fetched the latest Radio Times and a highlighter pen, allowing herself a grim smirk at the now pointlessness of this particular task.

She'd have a look anyway though out of curiosity, tutting at the evening's particularly thin schedule, flicking through the pages to the satellite channels that she didn't even subscribe to.

Back to the terrestrial choices and her pink nib hovered over an episode of a passable sitcom, one she had seen countless times and knew every joke verbatim, but she replaced the lid with a click, leaving the page unmarked.

A pot of tea and three custard creams sat on a small floral melamine serving tray on her coffee table. Next to it was her half-written letter to the historical society's chairman It said that she would be resigning her membership in view of the events around today's jubilee dinner – with the main issues set out in the form of bullet points in scale of escalating significance.

- PATRONISED BY the 'GIRL' FRIEND OF CURRENT CHAIRMAN
- DISRESPECTED over the seating arrangements.
- WRONG name on name plate.
- MARGINALISED by seating arrangement
- CONCERNED over diminishing standard of debate and conversation......
- INSULTED by seating arrangements

The list could have run and run with gripes, from the poor

English of the waiting staff to the lack of soft drink options but she knew to keep things succinct for more impact.

What started as an outlet for likeminded history enthusiasts to share their knowledge and interest has deteriorated to such an extent that it has become a society I barely recognise. From what I observed today, the event – one I had been looking forward to for some time – seemed little more than an opportunity for a drink and gossip as opposed to meaningful conversation which in the golden jubilee year of our majesty the queen is unforgivable. It goes without saying that I feel very offended and badly let down by everyone concerned.

She reread it a few times and made some grammatical tweaks and got up to fetch the thesaurus before sitting down again, tossing the notelet on the floor.

"Oh, what's the point."

She waited impatiently for the tea to stew before pouring the liquid through the strainer and tapping the residual dark mound of leaves into its matching drip tray. A long, satisfying sip followed, an audible hmmmm escaping as the rich, loose tea blend at just the right strength did the job; she'd miss this she thought briefly.

Now she bit half of the custard cream relishing the comforting and subtle vanilla hit which helped to mask the bitterness of the 18 crushed paracetamol which were slipping down surprisingly easy.

25

Maltham, England 2018

Sat on a stool confidently eyeing the camera, Leah Chase's image dominated the frontpage, an eye-catching splash of promise and glamour next to the grey headlines on interest rates. Wearing jeans and a coral pink top, her hair was in a ponytail, some deft lighting accentuated her high cheekbones.

The words below said:

Leah Chase was lighting a candle in a French church when she saw a familiar face in a crumpled photograph. What happened next would crack a fifteen-year-old mystery that stumped the most determined sleuths on both sides of the channel. Read her exclusive account of the Red Shoe case inside.

Ros Cowley settled in her usual spot on the sagging couch, fat fingers flicking through the pages expectantly, her cat next to her mirroring her line of focus.

Her eyes fell on the images of Jacque Renard in rural France alongside the more groomed four-year-old version in his school uniform in England a look she remembered well, and she briefly looked ahead at the mantle piece with its familiar trinkets and then outside in the garden where her young nephews were playing and signed deeply.

Another recent shot of Leah Chase saw her outside St Jean du Ruel church, hands in pockets leaning against the side of the stone wall, alongside another when she was a new reporter at in 2002 covering a vintage car rally.

For the purposes of this feature, Leah's sacking from a national paper, which Ros remembered from local gossip had undergone a favourable spin. The saga had been framed as clash between the prodigious and unappreciated talent of a woman at odds with the politics and cronyism of the newsroom she had found herself in.

Her desire to revisit a mystery that started as a young reporter on her local rag demanded a return to her old stomping ground away from the cut and thrust of Fleet Street. This not only made her appear dogged, dedicated and determined but seemed to have paid off professionally having secured a book deal which explored the mystery from her perspective with exclusive extracts to be published in the paper throughout the week.

"Getting back to the small community of Maltham and its secrets has been both cathartic professionally and personally. I had never expected to unearth what I did but of course, this is only a part closure on the whole affair. It doesn't give me any great pleasure in seeing David and Carolyn Steadman in prison, but justice had to be served. My next mission will be to get to the truth of what happened to Tom/Jacque once and for all."

Ros's little pin prick eyes devoured the copy quickly. It was compelling read packed with exclusives and fresh insight and witnesses who had never spoken on record before: A retired couple from Norfolk who had encountered David Steadman with the boy on the ferry when he was being brought over from

France and an anonymous ex pal of Carolyn Steadman who had long known that Carolyn wasn't the biological mother of Tom Steadman and had evidence to prove it.

The contributions were interspersed with the journalist's own musings in the wake of the Steadmans relatively modest sentences.

"So, what did *she* think had happened to Tom or Jacque Renard the interviewer asks in the final paragraph.

"I think if you'd asked me this a few years ago, my response would have been short and bleak because as an experienced hack I'm very much a realist, but now I feel as if nothing is impossible or off limits; there could still be another twist in the story."

The woman plucked the entire feature out of the magazine and removed the staples and took it into the kitchen and laid the pages across the floor in a large square.

She fetched her two pairs of her work shoes, a new purchase in honour of her latest promotion at the council that saw her now head of the communications team – on a fraction of the inflated salary of her old boss who had been a casualty of the latest round of redundancies.

Fetching the shoe polish and brushes from the cupboard, she dispensed a small smear on the shoe and began to brush briskly, small globs of wax dropping and smearing the words and pictures beneath. Afterward she inspected her handiwork and chucked the pages into the recycling bin.

ABOUT THE AUTHOR

Caroline Bullock is a Lancashire-born national journalist now based in West Sussex. Her journalism focuses on business news and interviews for The Times, Financial Times and Mail on Sunday as well as political and culture opinion commentary for the Daily Express, Daily Mail and New York Post.

The Missing Boy is her first novel. Inspired by her early career on local newspapers, her long term love affair with France and interest in cold case crime the mystery is rooted in the community, identity and personal redemption.